The Club

Hot Erotic Short Stories Illustrated with Hentai Pictures

_____

Emily White

TABLE OF CONTENTS

INTRODUCTION

Welcome to a captivating journey where my enthralling stories seamlessly intertwine with enchanting illustrations that redefine the very essence of desire in the world of hentai erotica.

Within the secret pages of these forbidden tales, I invite you to immerse yourself in a fiery universe of unrestrained passion. Every word is a whispered moan, and each illustration is a visual embrace that transforms the realms of fantasy into tangible reality.

This collection is not for the faint of heart. It's a bold manifesto, an invitation urging you to delve into the dark depths of lust, where pleasure is painted with audacious strokes and details that promise to quicken the rhythm of your heart. The illustrations are provocative gateways, guiding you into sensual dimensions where every hidden desire finds its expression without remorse.

Are you ready to plunge into a whirlwind of seduction and temptation, where the pages themselves transform into a stage for your most secret fantasies? Allow yourself to be carried away into a realm where sin transforms into art, and art seamlessly merges harmoniously with the ecstasy of desire.

Lift the cover and prepare for an experience ignited by the flame of passion. This is not just another collection; it's your exclusive ticket to the boldest manifestations of anime eros, written masterfully by me, **Emily White**.

THE CLUB

CHAPTER 1

Amandine Blenon hung up her phone, shaking. She had just spent almost an hour talking to her lawyer, and what he had revealed had shocked her. In just a few days, this beautiful 37-year-old woman's entire life seemed to fall apart. Married to the owner of one of the region's most successful restaurant chains, with whom she had two daughters, she thought she was financially secure, but now she knew she was deluding herself. Her husband had obviously gone into business with a con man in an obscure scheme that he thought would make him a fortune, but had actually swallowed up all of their assets. Worse, he found himself charged with embezzlement and breach of trust with several of his friends whom he had obviously scammed in an attempt to get himself out of trouble. He had admitted nothing to her and the worst part was that he was now on the run, leaving her alone to face creditors who were threatening to seize all their assets, including restaurants but also the beautiful home they lived in and shared with her sister's family who had just had a baby.

Amandine poured herself a well chilled glass of vodka to digest all the information she had just been told and drank it while looking at the creek that was below her house. They lived in a remote place a few miles from the city by the sea and this place was worth over two million. She couldn't understand how Jerome, her husband, could be involved in such a deal when they didn't need the money.

A ringing of the bell brought her out of her dark thoughts. It was the intercom at the entrance to the property. Someone was trying to get in. She pressed the button and the face of a blond man she didn't know appeared.

- Yes," she said. What do you want?

- My name is David Angel," the man replied with a smile. I have been associated with your husband and....

- I don't know where he is,' she replied, 'and if you insist I'll call security.

She was now used to being harassed by people who had been scammed by Jerome and his scammer friend. They would call her on the phone to ask for the money they had lost, to insult her or even threaten them and some of them had been bold enough to come over but fortunately the entrance to the property was protected by a large metal gate and she could contact private security who intervened in less than 10 minutes.

She wanted to disconnect the call but the man wouldn't give up.

- You are wrong, I am not a victim of your husband even though I know your problems. In fact, I am the solution.

He remained motionless, his finger inches from the intercom button, trying to pierce the expression of this stranger who was simply smiling. She didn't know him, but she remembered that Jeremy had already told her about a certain Angel he'd been associated with on a recent project, and he'd spoken nothing but good things about him. According to him, he was very wealthy. Maybe Jerome was using him to pass on a message to her. She wanted to believe that her husband hadn't completely abandoned her and her daughters. She took the opportunity and opened the door.

Angel arrived home five minutes later. Amandine opened the door for him and he looked surprised.

- 'I gave the whole staff the day off because of our...problems,' he explained in response to her silent question.

- I get it. What about your family?

- My sister and brother-in-law took my daughters out for the day to give me more time to talk to the lawyers.

- So we're on our own, you understand. It's perfect for what we need to talk about.

- Do you have any information about my husband," Amandine asked anxiously.

- Not exactly, could we discuss this somewhere more appropriate?

He led the way into the living room. He sat on the three-seater sofa while she sat on the single sofa across from him. A small glass coffee table separated them.

- Listening. What did you want to talk to me about?

- Like I said, I know about the cruel situation your husband left you in. The list of people who want money from you is impressive.

- They want it from my husband.

- Maybe, but you're married in the community, so his debts are yours too.

- I know. If you came to remind me of this, it was for nothing. My lawyer and my banker are here for that.

- In fact, they must not have told you that someone bought all your debts.

- And who would this person be?

- That would be me.

- You? But that's a huge amount of money.

- If you count the amounts I had to pay to appease the people who wanted to sue you, it's no less than 12 million, but your debts are only 6. So if I summarize, you owe me 8 million and I had all your assets appraised, and that's a long way off.

Amandine remained silent in front of this man who had simply given substance to all her problems.

- Reassure yourself," she continued, facing his silence. I am not as desperate as the poor people your husband has swindled to try to pay his debts. But I am demanding, and I can offer you a way out that could save your family.

- A way out?" she asked, both curious and anxious.

- I know your husband told you about me, he must have mentioned that I am an art lover since we met at an exhibition. In fact, I love all things beautiful, including beautiful women, and you are a very beautiful woman, Mrs. Blenon. I would be ready to forget all your debts if you would agree to obey me.

Indignant, Amandine rose from her seat and shouted.

- You are making fun of me, scum. You think I'm a cheap whore. Besides, what proof do I have that what I'm saying is not a pack of lies?

A cynical smile appeared on Angel's face as he picked up the briefcase he had brought with him.

- I thought you would doubt me," he said as he opened the briefcase. Here are all the termination deeds that prove that I have become your sole creditor. And given your reaction, I also want to show you this, which I discovered when I was searching for all of your husband's victims.

Amandine's anger had vanished in the face of Angel's impassivity. She sat down and picked up the papers he had placed on the table. She was not an expert and planned to show them to her lawyer to make sure they were authentic, but they left no doubt. The second stack of documents was different, they were notarized deeds and she noticed that they were signed by all the members of her family, her parents, her sister, her brother-in-law and of course herself.

- I can explain if you want. In the course of his "activity", your husband needed assistance, in fact the named but for the law are accomplices who are all equally guilty before the law. These accomplices are the people who signed these documents.

Amandine took these documents, especially the ones with her personal signature. She couldn't even remember where or when she signed them, but she trusted her husband so much that she could have done it.

- This means that if these documents make it to court, you and your entire family will be prosecuted for misuse of company assets. You may be able to prove your good faith, which is far from certain since you all benefited from the proceeds of your husband's scams, but you will face the consequences of an expensive trial. Think about your children. Your oldest daughter, Laura, is 18 and safe, but your youngest daughter, Maria, is 11 and still very fragile, especially if she is placed in a nursing home. She's not used to it and then there's your sister's baby, she's only a few months old and may not have any memory of her parents, that would be sad.

- Bastard! This time Amandine got angry. Go away. I never want to see you again!

Still calm as ever, Angel stood up. He put a small card on the glass table.

- All right, I'll let you think about it. Here's my card; contact me if you change your mind.

- Get out!!!!!!

Angel walked out with a smile on his face.

***

The next few days were hell. Her attorney and a notary public notarized Angel's documents and confirmed the reality that she and her family were now in danger of being sued. Worse, two days after this scum's visit, she was the victim of a police search and a summons from the judge who was investigating her husband's case, who told her that many of the victims had decided to file a complaint against her for compensation. Her lawyer reassured her by saying that in the current state of the investigation she was not risking anything but did not hide from her that if ever the documents she had shown him the day before arrived on the judge's desk, it would be immediate custody.

She realized then that Angel was setting a trap for her and that she had fallen into it. He would strip her mercilessly and then cause the downfall of her entire family. This little day was just a warning.

She spent a horrible night, not daring to admit to anyone the drama she was experiencing. In the morning she realized she had no choice and took Angel's card.

- Ms. Blenon," Angel said into the phone. I am happy to hear from you. I heard about your new misadventure, I'm sorry.

This answer confirmed Amandine's doubts but it was too late, she was trapped.

- I thought about your proposal. I accept it on condition that...

- It's not that simple," Angel interrupted her. 'If you had accepted right away, we could have negotiated the conditions, but now you made me wait and I hate waiting, so I want more to save your family. I also want Laura.

Amandine was struck by the man's arrogance and hung up, but immediately her phone rang and she knew it was him. Like a robot, he picked up.

- 'Don't ever do that again,' he said in an imperious tone, 'or your whole family will be in police custody within the day. I don't have time to play this game of cat and mouse anymore. Here's the deal: you will sell me your house and you and your daughter will stay there in my complete service. In return, I will offer your sister and her family a place to stay and your youngest daughter can go live with her grandparents. Everyone will return to the life they had before this sad affair. If you refuse, all the victims of your husband's fraud will wake up from their lethargy and the judge will receive the documents I have in my possession. There is no time to think, I want an answer now.

- I can't make a decision for my daughter, she is....

- It's up to you to convince her, remember it's your whole family and know that I have no mercy in business.

Amandine realized that she was defeated. She realized that she had to accept the diktat of this monster.

- I accept.

- This is good. I know it will take you some time to convince Laura, but if she's as sensitive as you are, you won't have much trouble either. I'll give you three days at the most. If you get there before then, let's agree on a signal.

I want you to lay out two pairs of panties, one belonging to you and one belonging to Laura, outside your door. Then you'll make sure you're alone for the evening and I'll come see you to seal our agreement.

He hung up, leaving Amandine alone with her despair.

***

Convincing Laura was the most terrible moment of Amandine's life. Laura was a young woman of 18 who would be graduating from high school in a few months and physically the opposite of her mother. She had dark hair, while her mother was blonde, and had very rounded, not to mention provocative, curves, unlike Amandine, whose model size drove the other mothers she met crazy. Laura was aware, much more than Maria thankfully, of the dire situation their family was in but she had never met Angel and did not understand the danger he posed to the three of them. To her mother's terrible dismay, the argument that tipped the scales was when she realized that she might soon be left in total destitution.

- 'It can't be as bad as you say,' said Laura. 'Maybe we can talk to him after all.

Amandine realized that her daughter was imagining that she could seduce this man to keep everything they had at her expense. To her shame, she did not let her illusions die; she needed his support too much. He had to sacrifice her to save everyone else.

Even though she had managed to convince Laura on the second day, Amandine allowed herself all the respite Angel had offered her. And on the morning of the third day, she asked Laura for one of her panties and laid it with one of her own in front of the mansion door. Paul, her brother-in-law, walked by and looked at her surprised but said nothing.

She had just finished when a message arrived on her cell phone.

"Tonight! 21h! You must be alone! Leave your panties where they are!

And he realized that Angel never stopped spying on them.

Convincing the rest of the family to leave wasn't easy but in the end she succeeded. Amandine had said that Laura was so sick about her father's problems that she wanted to talk to her alone.

At 9pm, there was a knock on the door. Angel had also managed to get the code of the gate of the property, Amandine realized, terrified. Like an automaton, he went to the entrance to open it.

In reality, he was a handsome bastard and she didn't understand why such a man would use such means to achieve his goals.

- Is Laura here?" she asked without even saying good evening.

- She's waiting in the living room," he answered as if in a nightmare.

- Perfect, I'll follow you.

He had given up on being polite. After all, he had understood, he had agreed to become her thing so he could accept it. She could feel his gaze wander over her as they made their way to the living room and she felt like throwing up.

Laura was sitting on one of the single couches. Amandine, still in shock from the horrible situation, sat on the other couch next to her daughter while Angel sat quietly in the middle of the three-seater couch in front of them.

- I'm happy to see you again, Laura. We met some time ago and that's when I met your father. You probably don't remember because you were having such a good time fluttering around all evening.

- But I do, Mr. Angel," Laura began in her game of seduction that worked so well on young people of her age.

- Master", Angel interrupted her with an abrupt and cold tone.

- I beg your pardon," said the young woman.

- From now on you will call me Master", he continued, still cold. Is that clear?

Laura's eyes swelled and she stared at Angel. She plunged her cold, hard gaze into his. It only took a few seconds for the girl's will to shatter like glass.

- 'Yes, Master,' Laura replied and Amandine's blood ran cold in her veins at her daughter's surrender.

***

Angel savored this easy victory. Laura Blenon had obviously thought he was one of her know-it-all kids who would be softened by her little antics. All she had to do was show him the utter futility of her tactics to crush him. Breaking his mother had obviously required more work and now he intended to take full advantage of it by starting with the amuse-bouches.

- I'm glad you've figured out your place," he said, taking advantage of the young adult's disconsolate expression. Get up!

His tone was so commanding that she stood up as if by reflex. Out of the corner of her eye, she also savored her mother's expression of dismay as she discovered how weak her daughter was.

- You are beautiful Laura, no doubt, but I want to see more. Take off that blouse.

This time she hesitated, but once again he looked into her eyes. The duel lasted only a moment and the girl's hands began to unfasten the buttons of the garment that she slid down her back.

Underneath she wore a simple white bra that barely hid her ample breasts.

- They must feel trapped in there, right? she said with a smile. Breasts need to breathe.

To her surprise, Laura didn't even wait for his order and immediately removed her bra. This girl's willpower was definitely not up to par. She was still whistling those two impressive breasts.

- They are really beautiful. How big do you think they are?

- Very big, she replied.

- Well, come over here.

Docile, the girl stepped over the coffee table to find herself in front of him. With a gesture of his finger he told her to kneel down. She did so and he began to touch her breasts.

- And also perfectly natural, he loved it, making sure his mother didn't miss anything in this little game.

The purpose of all this was obviously to humiliate Amandine as much as possible. Out of the corner of his eye, he could see her sinking into his couch as he debased his daughter before his eyes.

- 'I'm not forgetting about you, Amandine, don't worry,' he told her. 'Don't think I'm a sucker for big breasts. I know that even small ones have their charms, if only you would show us yours.

CHAPTER 2

Almost relieved that she was no longer a spectator, Amandine stood up and lifted the shirt she was wearing. She had obviously decided to challenge him by dressing in the least provocative way possible. A white t-shirt and faded jeans. Underneath, she wore no bra at all and her 85B appeared almost like a challenge. Angel preferred this position, he liked it when he was resisted, even defeated, he could still find the motivation to crush the remnants of will in his victim.

- You're right, Amandine, underwear is useless for women like you and from now on you won't wear it anymore.

She remained silent in the face of this new humiliation, but he wasn't finished.

- Did you understand?

- Yes, I understand.

- Yes, who?

- Yes, master.

That last word had almost ripped his tongue out and he took great pleasure in it. She pretended to approach them but he glared at her.

- Did I allow you to move? Stay where you are!

She remained motionless, arms fluttering, shirtless, while he turned his attention to Laura, whose breasts he still held in his hand. He realized his gaze was on her crotch. The little tussle with Amandine had turned him on terribly and an erection was now gripping him. It was time to spice up the game.

- Undo my pants and do your job.

Obediently, Laura unbuckled his belt and fly to pull out his already erect member. With the experience of a young girl who had already been practicing these oral games for a few years, she inserted her penis without reluctance to begin fellatio. Feeling the girl's tongue gently wander over his member, Angel realized that he would have little instruction to give her for now. Of course, the current young man was really aware of these phallic adventures and didn't know if he should rejoice or deplore. Either way, the pleasure was slowly building and he grabbed her by the hair to force her to slow down. There was no way she was going to make him cum too fast, the little jerk. He wasn't one of those inexperienced teenagers she was used to messing with, he wanted so much more. Still frighteningly docile, she complied with the speed he was imposing on her. Halfway through her pleasure, she continued to enjoy intensely the vision of Amandine watching in horror as her daughter engaged in acts worthy of the last of the whores.

- And this is only the beginning, he thought. You will see much more tonight, love, and only then will I fuck you.

When he thought Laura had used her mouth enough, he had her stand up.

- Take off my pants," he ordered.

She did so and, again anticipating his orders, took off her panties as well. He rewarded her with a masterful slap. Amandine wanted to go on but he straightened up and with a look he made her understand that if she made a move, she would be welcomed in the same way.

- Here, I am the only one who makes decisions and none of you are to do anything without my order, he explained.

It wasn't about reversing roles and making the slave the master of the game, and he liked to inflict punishment.

- Do you understand this rule? Answer me!!!

- Yes, master," said Laura, docile as always.

- Yes... master," said Amandine who resisted a little longer before giving up.

- Very good, Laura. Now it's your turn to get your ass naked.

The young girl, her cheek still red from the slap she had just received, didn't hesitate to take off the dress she had put on when she still thought she could seduce this stranger, the lace thong followed her immediately. Angel then had her lie on her back on the coffee table and sank his head into her intimacy. Not that he really intended to give her pleasure, that wasn't on the agenda for this evening; no, he just wanted to test a hypothesis he had made based on the actions of this little slut.

- 'Your daughter is as wet as the last whore,' he told Amandine, who winced at this news. And of course she is no longer a virgin. At what age did you let yourself be taken for the first time?

- This year," she answered.

Angel then smiled and violently pinched her clitoris. Laura squealed and Angel was happy to see that this time Amanda hadn't made a move.

- Don't lie to me, I can't stand it.

And again he pinched her, making her scream even louder. This time Amanda didn't hold back and wanted to get closer. Angel pinched her even harder and this time she screamed.

- If you move again," he told her, "next time I'll pinch her with my teeth and her screams will be heard all over the gulf.

Amandine's face broke; he realized she was wondering if she would be able to stop him from carrying out his threat. When he saw her arms come down his body again, he knew he had won again.

- So I asked you a question, you little bitch, and this time don't lie to me.

- At 16," Laura complained, suddenly seeming to find the game less fun.

- I knew it, you've just been freed from the family yoke and you're starting to do anything. That's fine, at least your pussy will be nice and cozy.

He grabbed her by the hair and forced her to kneel on the couch.

- Get your ass up!

As a result of her large breasts, her buttocks were wider, something Angel hated, and she was already thinking about the pleasure she would get from exploring her tight little ass. Still in tears, Laura performed, exposing both her anus and her vulva to the sight of the man who had become her master. For a moment she thought about attacking the only virginity she had left, but she had promised to reserve it for someone else. Then she settled for planting his penis, whose erection had been maintained by the abuse he had just inflicted on her, into her sex. The pain was far from drying up and he entered with an ease that almost ruined her pleasure. Very quickly the little slut began to pant under his thrusts and he realized that she must not be used to being fucked by a real man, that would change. As he increased the pace, he could hear her screaming louder and louder, and out of the corner of his eye, he was also enjoying the sight of his mother devastated to see her taking such pleasure in being raped. She wasn't losing her sense of reality.

- Amandine, she said, these jeans are horrible, take them off!

Realizing that her turn would come soon, Amandine immediately removed her pants. She had learned her daughter's lesson, because she didn't overdo it and kept the little white panties she was wearing.

- No underwear, she said, as the pleasure of fucking the girl began to mount dangerously.

She shed her panties and he withdrew from Laura, who moaned in annoyance.

- 'Let's get to work,' he said as he approached Amandine.

Like her daughter, the mother found herself exposed with her ass in the air.

- You see, Laura. If your mother doesn't have a chest as slutty as yours, she makes up for it with the best ass in town.

She slipped two fingers into Amandine's vulva and discovered that, unlike her daughter, her mother was as dry as the Gobi Desert.

- 'Fortunately my cock is well impregnated with your daughter's moisture,' he said, knowing that this would only add to the humiliation of this woman he longed to crush.

Without further ado, he thrust into her, eliciting a cry very different from Laura's moans of pleasure. Amandine's hands tightened on the skin of the couch as she was raped for the first time by this man who had decided to enslave her. Angel was enjoying this second penetration immensely more. He was thrusting in and out of her, slowing the pace until she thought he was about to come out, only to suddenly come out again, eliciting more screams from her. Yet he could also feel her pussy gradually becoming wetter, and he knew that this alone would increase the sense of disgust she would feel tomorrow. He was almost cumming inside her when he finally pulled out because he wanted icing on the cake.

Amandine was curled up on the couch, crying, and he was standing behind her, his cock in his hands. He had forgotten about

Laura, who was sitting naked on the three-seater couch, waiting for him to do his bidding and watching his mother's rape.

- 'I'm not finished,' he said imperiously. Get back in position!

Shocked, Amandine did not react. A slap hit her right buttock, followed immediately by another on her left buttock but she still remained in the fetal position. Then Angel's gaze returned to an object in the right corner of the room.

Despite her state, Amandine noticed it and did the same and realized that she had noticed the poker that was by the fireplace. Her blood ran cold and before Angel could make a move towards the fireplace, she straightened up to resume her stance, ready for a second round.

Except Angel had no intention of fucking her. Again two fingers explored one of her slits but it was her asshole. She screamed; she wanted to escape but he slammed her head against the back of the couch.

She almost choked when she felt his glans press against the halo of her anus. But she stubbornly resisted and he couldn't get her to stay still and properly position the tip of his penis at the same time, so he dared the unthinkable.

- Laura! Come here!

With her head buried in the leather of the sofa, Amandine could not see her daughter approaching. Angel doubted that her daughter's strength would be enough to hold back the mother who was resisting like a fury. So she opted for another tactic.

- You're going to drive my cock straight into your mother's ass!

Laura was speechless.

- Do it!

Once again she surrendered to the new authority that had come over her. And her hands went to Angel's cock. Amandine then felt a force pressing against her anus in a pressing way and finally a horrible pain tore her insides. Angel had succeeded in his endeavor, he was fucking her.

However, he could not doubt the virginity of this superb ass that had made him dream so much so his cock, of a more than consequential size also, found himself caught as if in a vice and despite his efforts echoed by the cries of pain of his victim, he managed to penetrate it only a few inches. However, he persisted for long moments that seemed an eternity to the unfortunate Amandine.

- Enough!!! She screamed. Enough!!! I'll give you anything you want but please stop!!!!

"But you have no choice," Angel thought. "And you'll give me more than you think you're capable of, believe me. But right now, he deprived himself of the pleasure of revealing this truth to her in order to take advantage of this new abandonment on her part. He intended to use it to derive at least one last true pleasure from this lesson-filled evening.

- Very well," he breathed into her neck. So in return you will offer me a pleasure that until now you have offered only to your husband: I will come inside you.

She remained silent and to overcome her last reluctance, he gave a new blow of his kidneys, his member sank a new inch into her bowels tearing her a new howl.

- Aaahhhhhhhhhh!!!! Yes, okay," she folded. Come inside me!

Then he pulled out of her anus and forced her to turn around. He wanted to read the disgust and shame in her eyes as he cum inside her.

He planted himself inside her. With his hands, he forced her to look into his eyes as he worked her. He saw tears in the corners of her eyes and this last sight brought him to ecstasy. Two jets of cum then flooded the vaginal cavity of this superb middle-class woman, completing the humiliation.

His member still pulled up, Angel then grabbed Laura who was still kneeling a few inches from them and forced her to lick the mixture of cum and wetness dripping from it. As the girl finished satisfying the last vestiges of her manhood, she turned to her mother.

- Who knows, maybe tonight we conceived a little brother for the little slut you have.

And she gave a laugh that ended one of her best evenings in a long time.

CHAPTER 3

Half an hour after enjoying Amadine's body to the fullest, Angel dismissed Laura to be alone with his mother whom he had seated on one of the couches. If he had dressed, he had told her to remain completely naked; even if it was no longer about fucking her, he had no intention of depriving himself of some small pleasure. In fact, he was prolonging his presence in this house to sort out some essential details that couldn't wait.

- Sign this," he ordered, handing her several documents.

She stared at him with a puppy dog look that might have softened
him if he had a heart. She was still in shock at what he had just

done to her and didn't quite understand what was happening to her.

- These are the termination papers for the house. I want your sister and her family out by the end of the week.

Still looking like a whipped dog, the urge to slap her across the face crossed his mind but he doubted the effectiveness of that method; even he had to show a little tact now and then.

- They'll surely hate you, he admitted, but they'll soon forget when they find out where they're going to live from now on.

He saw a small glimmer of hope appear in her eyes; it was something, but the worst was yet to come.

- This is a certificate to the juvenile judge that you are relinquishing your parental authority over Maria to your father. A friend has already arranged to expedite the process, so you can move out – again before the end of the week.

- Maria – gone – said, "before the end of the week?

- Unless you want her to attend the next such parties I plan to throw, or attend them?

This last argument came as a shock, Amandine took her pen and signed immediately. Angel was convinced that the child would be at her grandfather's the next day. He could leave in peace; a good part of his contract had already been fulfilled.

***

Sitting in the back of his car, Angel smiled as they drove past Amandine's small family vehicle. They had no idea of the nasty surprise that awaited them.

The businessman nodded to his driver and he raised the partition window. He took out his phone to contact one of the other members of the club.

- Hi Judge," he said, "the little operation went off without a hitch. I'll send you the surrender papers in the morning as scheduled.

- Superb," his caller replied, "you must be pleased.

- And you will be too. Laura is just as you like her, young, beautiful and surprisingly docile. As agreed, I have saved her anal grommet for you.

- You are worthy of the club," said the judge. I'll see you at the meeting," he added before hanging up.

Angel did the same, smiling. The Club had changed his life.

It was a very select group of men who had gathered around very specific interests. A group of four very rich and powerful men who had met by chance. In fact, none of them could say exactly what had led them to form the club. Despite their wealth, they were not all in the spheres.

Angel was a stranger in this small region. He had become a billionaire through new technologies and had continued to prosper in various businesses, but eventually he had become so jaded that he had left the management of the bulk of his financial group to underlings who were content to keep him alive. He had undertaken dozens of adventurous challenges around the world, but even the adventurousness had become tiresome and he was a bored thirty-something who found himself in this region with the impression that his life was over when it had just begun. The club had changed that.

The Honorable Judge Jules De Saint Servier was an entirely different character, by far the oldest member of the club. He was an influential notable, a judge and officially a second-rate politician, but in reality the real mastermind behind the right-wing party that was in power in the region, and he was one of the most powerful men in the area. On the surface, he was a man at ease with himself, but in reality he was a giant who complained about having to live among the ants, forced to limit his desires because of the psychoriginal upbringing he had undergone. The club had opened new horizons for him and allowed him to finally dare to abuse the immense power he possessed for the sole purpose of satisfying his boundless perversion.

Guillaume Uron was the youngest member of the club. He was the youngest son of one of the region's greatest fortunes and its greatest shame. Alcohol, drugs, women and other morally reprehensible pleasures, there was nothing Uron's young son hadn't tried to the point that his father had totally disinherited him for the sole benefit of his eldest son... but it was without counting the providence that after his father's natural death, a tragic car accident led to that of his brother and the entire family. Uron ended up becoming a millionaire and seemingly settled down. Apparently only because in reality his efficiency and determination had attracted the attention of club members who offered him a new and more suitable playground.

The last member of the club was Guillermo Diaz and unlike the previous ones, he was not from high society. He was an immigrant who had started his life working on construction sites, but he was also a man of rare intelligence who, by dint of determination, had managed to forge an empire in the service world. Now, the simple worker commanded a vast network that provided hundreds of home services, from cleaning to teaching, to thousands of clients. A veritable small army of little servants dedicated to satisfying the wealthiest of regional society... and many little spies who formed an inexhaustible mine of information to uncover all their most unmentionable secrets.

As Angel had already said, the club had changed all their lives because it had revealed a reality. They were rich and powerful and yet they all felt constrained, tired, for the simple reason that this world was too small for them. So they had decided to push the boundaries and enjoy all the pleasures that life had to offer, because if they were powerful, there was still so much to do in this region and they would only be satisfied when they held the region in the palm of their hands. And then there was sex.

They had never had a problem with women, money and power were powerful aphrodisiacs, but that was no longer enough for them; they wanted more. Now they wanted more absolute pleasures with less accessible women. Chasing a woman like prey on a hunt to finally force her to surrender everything to them without any limits: that was their total pleasure.

To officially seal the birth of the club, which for the time being was a simple group of friends, they had decided to open their herd of victims. Each member of the group was given a list of three victims to degrade. He was to choose two of the names himself and one of the other members would dictate the third. The rules were simple: no direct violence (don't brutalize them to force them to obey you) and don't buy them; that would be too easy. Otherwise, all tricks were allowed: blackmail, lies, and other shenanigans. Once the 12 victims have been captured, the club will gather to celebrate with dignity.

Angel looked at his personal list. He could cross off the two names of Amandine and Laura Blenon, Laura having been his "imposed figure" by the judge. He turned his attention to the third name: Christine Veron.

It was a quiet day at the hostel. It was there that Christine, 31, had worked for years as a specialized educator. Her job was to help the people who lived there with their administrative procedures, their search for work or housing, or simply to guide them when they crossed certain boundaries or experienced dangerous lows. The people who lived there, men and women of all ages in a precarious situation, often needed all of this and it was often exhausting. On this day, however, the center was very quiet. It was the weekend and she was on duty. These long days were hard on this young woman who often had to spend them alone, waiting in a center emptied of its residents who only returned in the evening. Fortunately, she knew that soon she would no longer have to deal with such obligations, as she would soon be appointed to the position of director of the center. One might think she was very young to hold such a position, but when you are the daughter of Jacques Veron, the recently deceased founder of the Lilleland region's homeless shelter network, and when you have put your heart and soul into your work since leaving school nearly a decade ago, you don't think this honor comes too soon.

The doorbell rang and the voice of a man she didn't know told her he wanted to apply for a position at the center. She opened the door and saw a man walking up the stairs to her office. For the sake of discretion, she closed the door behind him and sat him down at his desk before sitting down across from him.

Strangely enough, he felt uncomfortable in this man's presence, as he looked nothing like the regulars of this place. He was certainly not dressed smartly, but everything about his demeanor indicated that he came from a much more affluent background than he wanted her to believe. He felt the anxiety of being confronted with a sick person when he was unassisted. However, the man showed no signs of nervousness.

- Hello," he said, trying to hide his apprehension as best he could. What can I do for you?

-As I said, I'm in a delicate situation. The person who housed me for some time just kicked me out and now I'm homeless and have nowhere to go. A friend told me I could come here.

- 'Yes, of course,' said Christine, who relaxed at this talk she knew all too well. 'We'll see what we can do for you but first I need some information. Do you have an ID card?

The man took out a small envelope and put it on the table.

- It's all there," he said laconically.

CHAPTER 4

Madeleine reappeared in Jerome's apartment in a terrible state, and the young delinquent knew at once that the old pervert of a judge had had his fun with this little crane. He had drawn features and dark circles around his eyes that indicated he had been crying his eyes out. Worse, he immediately noticed his unusual arched gait, which showed that the old man had come down the fire escape. He held back a smile when he realized what this saintly woman had been willing to accept when she had previously been so reluctant to the most basic of caresses. She certainly had a lot to learn from the judge and his methods of manipulation.

- Sit down," he said, falsely sympathetic. Now it was over.

She had all the trouble in the world to find a sitting position that didn't make her feel like a martyr, but Jerome couldn't enjoy the show too much, the only pleasure he could still get from Madeleine.

He turned to the judge's driver who handed him a package that was supposed to be payment for Madeleine's "service." It was all fake, of course, but he had to play the game to the end. Suddenly he wondered if this mountain of muscle had attended the little party. The giant remained silent as usual and left as soon as his package was delivered.

Jeremy then turned his attention to Madeleine, who he felt was on the verge of a nervous breakdown. He needed to cheer her up a bit because if she collapsed now and her parents noticed, their plan might fail. He walked over to her and took her in his arms. She hugged him and started crying. He found this behavior ridiculously weak, but he knew it served him well. He stayed huddled against her for as long as it took. Eventually she wiped away his tears and he separated from her.

- I know it was terrible," she lied, "but you won't see him again. I will buy the goods and soon we will be free. I'll have to go away for a few days.

He immediately saw the panic in her eyes and realized how right the judge was.

Make yourself wanted," he explained. Make yourself rare and you will see that you will become indispensable. He applied his precepts and had to admit that his encounter with this perverse old man had really changed his life. From being a simple little punk with no future, he had become someone in the neighborhood thanks to his advice and the money he had already given him just because he had been lucky enough to seduce a girl that no one wanted because she was so boring. Even one of the queens of the neighborhood like Felicia, who in the past didn't even pay attention to him, preferring to be fucked by the big boys who drove her around in their big cars, now came running whenever he whistled.

Also, tonight, while the other bitch was getting her ass kicked by the judge, he was taking the opportunity to have sex with her. He had to get over his frustration because the judge had forbidden him to touch Madeleine, who was only asking for it.

- How long would this take? Madeleine asked anxiously. How long will I go without seeing you?

- I don't know," he replied. 'A week, maybe two.

That had to be vague enough to add to her confusion.

- 'Don't worry, I'll get back to you as soon as I can.'

He felt she was lost and it was time to strike the blow. He picked up the pipe he had made her smoke earlier and handed it to her.

- Here, smoke it, it will calm you down a bit.

Completely anxious, she took the pipe and quickly inhaled a puff of smoke. She knew immediately by the turned-up look on his face that the drug was working. It wasn't a strong dose, on the contrary; the judge had also forbidden him to make her an addict.

'If you take it enough to make her lose some sense of reality, that would be ideal,' he had explained, 'but no more. I don't want you to turn her into a wreck or make her too dependent. When the time comes, I want to be able to wean her off it.

***

The week that followed was a real ordeal for Madeleine. Jerome never heard from her again and not a second went by without her thinking of him or the horrible act she had to endure. She had nightmares every night, waking her sister who was sleeping in the next room. Jerome had left her a pipe and some doses to calm her anxieties but she had quickly used up her stash and now had nothing to protect her from the trauma of the horrors she had experienced. She needed Jerome more than ever.

He reappeared ten days after their previous meeting and she came downstairs to join him. Again she threw herself on him and kissed him. Once again he was distant, which drove her crazy.

- I'm glad to see you again," she said, her actions belying his words. I managed to retrieve the goods but it wasn't easy. I think I'm being watched by the police.

- The police? panicked.

- It's nothing serious. It's because of Joel, my roommate. They are watching the apartment and I can't take that many drugs with me, that would be crazy. I need a place to hide it. That's why I'm here, you have to keep it at home.

- My place? But I can't.

- I don't have anywhere else to hide it and I need time to monetize it. If you love me, you have to.

He held her close and once again she felt unable to resist him.

- Don't leave me alone anymore," she despaired, "I need you.

- We won't be separated anymore. I promise you that. Proof...

Then he gave her a small cell phone.

- It's a card phone," he explained. 'I just bought it. Only I have the number, don't give it to anyone. I'll call you every night, I promise.

She felt suddenly reassured at the mere idea of hearing from him every night and he handed her another small package.

- Here! It's some doses for your pipe...to keep you going.

She took the two packets and reluctantly went home after kissing him for a long time. When she returned to her room, she was surprised to find Sarah waiting for her.

- Damn it, Madeleine," she exclaimed. What are you playing at?

- Nothing, I just went to join Jeremy as usual.

- Don't. I can sense that you're not well.

She stared at her younger sister. She was only a year younger than her and, until a month ago, had been the person she felt closest to. Yet she was also the one she was most different from. Sarah resembled her physically, she was blonde like her, she always wore her hair in a ponytail and if their faces were similar, their bodies were different. Although younger, Sarah strangely looked more like a woman, but she was still nervous, immature, her mother thought. In fact, Madeleine seemed to be the head and Sarah the heart.

She wanted to tell him the truth, she was his sister, then she thought about what she had promised Jerome and decided to keep quiet.

- You're wrong, she lied. I'm perfectly fine. And now leave me alone!

Sarah opened her mouth, but she wouldn't let him and threw her out of the house. It was the first time she had been violent towards him since they were teenagers and she felt guilty.

***

Again, she did not see Jerome for several days. However, he kept his word by calling her every night on the phone he had left for her, but their conversations remained brief and frustrating: she wanted to see him and he refused for fear of jeopardizing their plan. She became more and more nervous, couldn't study, and used more and more of the smoking stuff. Then one day what was supposed to happen happened. Her mother cornered her in the kitchen for "an important conversation."

- Madeleine," she said, terribly serious. I'm worried. I just got a phone call from one of your teachers. He was very unhappy when he told me that your results were in free fall. He told me your next report card was going to be catastrophic.

He wondered who might be ratting him out. He didn't think that in one month his grades had gotten so bad that one of his teachers had contacted his mother directly. She had to do everything she could to keep her composure and not give herself away.

Her mother approached her and tried to take her hand. She did not refuse this contact so as not to alarm her. In the past she had always gotten along well with her, unlike Sarah who had often been on the outs with her.

- You know you can tell me anything," he assured her. 'If you have a problem, I can help you.

She hesitated for a moment before adding:

- If it's that little punk.

- 'He's not a hooligan,' she said, and realized that all her efforts to hide her nervousness had been in vain.

- 'I know very well what he is. He is a small-time dealer and a dirty drug dealer.

He stood in front of her and realized that she was trying to see if his pupils were red. He looked away for fear of revealing the truth.

- My God Madeleine...," her mother panicked. Your teacher was right.

- Right about what?! she shouted, both in anger and to end the conversation. What is she accusing me of? Selling drugs? Like you did with Jerome?

Her mother was speechless at these accusations and knew she had hit the nail on the head. She had indeed reported her boyfriend to the police. She ran off crying to her room. Her mother shouted for her to come back, also crying. She knew he was going to come after her, but the sound of the front doorbell saved her from continuing this horrible conversation. She thought she was safe-she didn't know she was falling from Scylla to Charybdis.

- Police, ma'am," said a loud voice. We're answering your call!

- My call..." her mother stammered.

Madeleine realized that the police were coming, that they would search her room and find the package of drugs. She was in a complete panic when a ringtone told her that she had just received a text message on Jerome's cell phone.

- Run! Run! repeated the message.

As if overwhelmed by this message, she jumped out the window and took the fire escape to escape, leaving everything behind. She ran through the streets with no destination, convinced that the cops would chase her. She galloped for almost 10 minutes and then, exhausted, stopped to catch her breath. Still in a state of panic, she set off again, wanting to reach Jerome's apartment, but then realizing that would be the first place her mother would point to the police. Completely lost, she wandered the streets for hours when the phone finally rang again. She answered the phone like a madwoman.

- Damn it," said Jerome's voice. I stopped by, it's full of cops.

- My God, Jerome, they knew everything. I had to run.

- Run away? But how? What about the cargo?

- Jerome, he shouted, I need you.

- Very well, very well! All right, then! Meet me at the south dock.

He ran back toward the dock. It took half an hour, but by the time he arrived Jerome was already there and he looked terribly nervous. She threw herself on him to seek comfort in his touch. He hugged her but quickly pulled away because he wanted to explain. She told him everything and as she did so, she saw his face crumble.

- What about the goods?" he finally asked. What did you do with it?

- I had to leave it. I took your advice and ran.

- My advice?

- Your advice? Your text message.

- I didn't text you anything. You panicked, yes. You should have brought the drugs with you, Madeleine.

- They were going to arrest me.

- But you don't understand me. I was supposed to sell some this afternoon and pay my suppliers tonight, I'm already two days late. Now that you've lost the stuff, I've got nothing. They're not jokers.

- We have to go...

At that moment, a big car appeared in the night and stopped a few meters away from them. Two two-meter tall behemoths got out. Madeleine immediately understood from Jerome's expression that he knew them and that they were not friends.

- Mr. Freddy wants his money, Jerome," said one of the gorillas, approaching.

- I'll explain," said Jerome.

But before he could say a word, he was punched in the face and fell to the ground. The gorilla who had hit him threw himself on top of him and kicked him, causing his nose to bleed. Madeleine ran screaming to get in the way, but the second gorilla grabbed her and despite her best efforts, she could not escape his iron grip.

- You owe us a lot of money and we won't tolerate any delays," said the gorilla who had hit Jerome. 'You have to pay us or else.

He hit him again and more blood spurted out. Madeleine screamed. The gorilla turned to her and pulled out a gun.

- Shut up, bitch, or I'll shut you up!

She fell silent, staring at the gun in horror, and the gorilla turned back to Jerome.

- What's that bitch's name?

- She's my girlfriend.

- That's not what I asked you.

- Madeleine Bonnet.

- You have two days. If not, we'll come back and see you both.

The second gorilla let go of Madeleine and she knelt beside Jerome whose face was smeared with blood. The car drove off into the night, leaving them alone.

CHAPTER 5

- Damn it," Jeremy sniffed, wiping his face. 'They're going to kill us both.

- We have to run," Madeleine suggested.

- You think it's so easy. We don't have a dime, and we can't run from people like that. I need that money.

Madeleine was losing her mind. She had seen those two goons and heard their threats. She knew they weren't kidding. She should never have let herself get involved in this.

- Can no one help us?

- The only person rich enough to get us out of all our problems is the judge.

A terrible chill ran through her body as she thought about the monster who had defiled her.

- He will never help me at all. He's not a good Samaritan, as you may have guessed. The only one who could convince him would be you.

His heart stopped beating and he couldn't utter a word.

- He enjoyed your meeting and might be willing to pay again.

- No!!! Never!!!!

He took her by the shoulders and looked her straight in the eyes. He could clearly see the damage the two gorillas had done to that beautiful face he adored.

- Madeleine, our lives are at stake. They will kill us or worse. Believe me, they are bullies and there are cops too. If they catch us, we'll be gone for life.

She would have rather died than let that rotten old man get his hands on her again, but there was Jerome, she didn't want him dead. Madeleine was losing her balance. She wished she could have pulled her pipe, which she had left in her room.

- Fine, she agreed and felt immediately nauseated.

***

Even though Jerome had called the judge in the middle of the night, he had finally answered. He had explained the situation to her and the judge had agreed to see Madeleine alone. It was agreed that her driver would pick her up at the port as soon as possible. They had to wait for almost two hours and finally the big white car arrived. It took immense efforts of will for Madeleine to get into this car that was taking her to hell. The car started without further ado and she drove in a daze through half the city.

She found the same building, the same elevator and the same hallway, a veritable antechamber to hell. All the way to the apartment door, she had leaned on the powerful arm of the driver who had remained perfectly impassive to her weaknesses.

When they arrived in the living room where she had been subjected to the worst of the abuse, they found the judge sitting on one of the couches, making a phone call. She looked at them but did not stop talking. Then he realized with horror that he was talking about her.

- I judged a case of the young man some time ago and I know the young woman from my past. It's really sad, she had a bright future. Keep me informed, my friend.

He hung up and returned his attention to her. With a glance, he dismissed the driver and once again she was alone with this monster, fully aware of how it would end.

***

- I just spoke to the bailiff in charge of investigating your deplorable trafficking," she stated as if she was unaware of the purpose of the money she had paid to abuse her body. The evidence is overwhelming for both you and him and the amount seized is frightening. Also, it sounds like you are a drug dealer and not a small-time dealer. If I don't do something, the sentence could be very heavy. And of course there's the money you owe dear Freddy, quite a sum.

- I..." she stammered, "I'm aware of that, and I'm ready to pay... like last time.

These last words had torn her tongue out but she had said them, there was no going back. However, the judge smiled wryly and stood up.

- No, you are not aware of anything, you little fool. The amount of money you are asking me to save your heads is ten times more than I paid last time. Besides, I would be obliged to compromise myself by intervening in your case. I would risk my position if this were noticed. If you think one night of sex will be enough to pay me back, you are way off base.

Madeleine found herself trapped. He had approached her and was staring at her with his brutal blue eyes.

- What do you want?" he said, realizing that she would have to give in to his demands.

- For you to stay here permanently.

This time it was too much. She started screaming and collapsed on the nearest couch. Her eyes filled with tears and she turned to face him.

- Mai! You're crazy!

As soon as she finished her sentence, he was on top of her and slapped her in the face.

- You don't understand a thing, you little bitch," he said, shaking her. One word from me and the police will come here and you'll find yourself convicted within a week. You think you've been through hell with me, wait till you see the prison I'll have you sent to, nothing but long sentences, bullies who will turn you into their little doll if they let you live. As for your boyfriend, I'd let Freddy take care of him and then I'd take care of Freddy, I've been waiting for an opportunity for so long.

Shaken like a plum, Madeleine understood the man's violence and his true power. She could save them or throw them into the void. She had condemned herself from the moment she had agreed to get in the car to join him, but she could still save Jerome.

- 'I'll do whatever you want,' she surrendered between sobs.

- Beautiful," thundered the judge.

He brought his face closer to hers and she thought he was going to kiss her like last time but he sniffed.

- You stink," he said. You're going to take a shower and change your clothes. Then we'll talk about your future life. Behind that door is a bedroom and adjacent to it is a bathroom with a shower. Use it!

She stood up like a zombie and headed for the door he had pointed to and found herself in a large room with two beds. On the opposite wall was a doorless opening to another room and she could clearly make out the shower. She turned on the water and took off her very dirty clothes, then slipped under the jet of hot water. Under other circumstances the strong current would have been a comfort but she couldn't find anything positive in her misery. She reached into the bath to clean herself when she felt a presence behind her. She wanted to turn around but it was too late, the judge grabbed her arm and slammed her hard against the wall. With his other hand, he forced her to lift her left leg as high as possible, clearing access to her groin.

He inserted himself into her without caution and began to file in. Chest pinned against the cold wall and under the surprise blow, she could only gasp under the blows of the old man who was struggling behind her. Full of ardor for a man her age, he besieged her under the spray for long minutes and then suddenly withdrew without cumming and she knew immediately what that meant. He pulled her away from the wall and forced her to bend forward.

- Get your ass up, you little whore," he ordered.

Subdued by the brutality of this man who now held her life in his hands, she arched her back as far as she could, the hot water running down her back to her neck. The judge inserted his hands between her buttocks to ensure the proper distance and she gritted her teeth in anticipation of the pain that would soon come.

But she couldn't hold back her screams as the column of flesh pierced her insides for the second time in her life. Not caring about her screams, the judge immediately went back outside, only to dive in again, causing her to scream again.

He repeated this act four times and then began filing her faster and faster and she screamed with an intensity she never thought herself capable of. Her eyes filled with tears, she was just waiting for the humiliating sensation of the judge's semen coming out to end her ordeal. But this time the judge hadn't decided to cum between her buttocks, so he got out and pulled her by the hair to bring her mouth to his cock.

She sniffed but opened her mouth to swallow; she was too afraid the judge would decide to repeat his sodomy. She sped up her fellatio to bring him to orgasm as quickly as possible, an act she had learned before meeting this monster. Then he jumped all over her face, smearing her hair and the top of her chest. Then he let go of her hair.

- Finish your shower," she said breathlessly.

Defeated, broken, she meekly obeyed.

When she finally got out of the shower, she found no trace of her clothes.

- I had them thrown away," the judge said from the room. Let's go!

Naked, she crossed the room and, at his command, came to sit on one of the two beds next to him.

- This one will be your bed. The other is reserved for a future resident who will soon be joining us.

He then pointed to the closet at the foot of his bed. He saw that it was locked.

- Your new clothes are there. Only I have the key to this closet, because you will only need clothes when we leave. You will be naked here all the time. Don't ever try to go out without my permission or I'll make sure your boyfriend pays his debt with his blood, is that clear?

- Yes, that is clear.

- Very good," he congratulated himself, playing with her nipples. You will see that we will be very happy together. Now go to bed! I want you to get some rest when I come back from court tomorrow.

***

The judge left Madeleine's room and locked it. He didn't want her to be able to hear the conversation he was about to have. He picked up his phone and dialed a number.

- Hello? Jerome?

- Judge," came the young man's voice. How did it go?

- Ideally. You will receive the deposit tomorrow. That way you'll be able to afford that car you've been dreaming about. You'll have to call her Madeleine.

The young man burst out laughing.

- But don't forget," the judge interrupted him. If you want the full amount, you'll have to give me the other package.

- It will be done.

The judge hung up and turned his attention to the closed door. He finally had the dream that had pursued him all his life without ever having the courage to realize it: a young slave who would fulfill all his fantasies as soon as he got home.

He was angry that he had only met the other members of the Club on the night of his life and that he had allowed the shackles of Christian morality to limit his life for so long, but fortunately that was all over now and he planned to make up for lost time.

He swallowed a small blue pill and headed for Madeleine's room. He would have all day tomorrow to rest, tonight he would have more work to do....

CHAPTER 6

The bay window opened onto a sunset that radiated its fiery light on a fine sandy beach that seemed to have no end. However, this idyllic sight was the least of poor Madeleine's worries. At this very moment she was on all fours on the carpet of this luxurious hotel room, the weight of the judge on her back and her sex frozen in her vagina. She was panting under the blows of the old man who, since they had arrived in Mexico, had not stopped fucking her in the most unusual places according to her desires, taking advantage of the anonymity she enjoyed abroad.

She gritted her teeth in disgust when she felt the heat of his semen flowing into her belly. He had confiscated her contraceptive pills for the past week and now she had to live with the fear of becoming pregnant by her tormentor. Even when he was full, the old man didn't release her and he weighed himself down on his back for a long time before getting up with an expression of ecstasy on his face that made him want to vomit. He sat on the couch a foot away and watched her for a few moments as she lay on the floor, trying to catch her breath.

- 'It's hot,' he said. 'You're sweaty. You need a good shower.'

He understood the implied order and struggled to his feet, heading for the bathroom, knowing full well how it would end. Soon the judge would slip behind her into the shower and sodomize her mercilessly. She held back tears as she cursed that damn Viagra that allowed that old man to be as active as a twenty year old.

The judge let Madeleine get in the shower and went to the mini-bar to pour herself a drink. He would wait a while before joining his beautiful slave. The idea that she would spend long minutes under the hot water in terror of apprehension was the beginning of his enjoyment. He sipped his drink as he watched the sun set and thought about the other reason he had chosen Mexico as his vacation destination.

***

Leo Campo, a lawyer at the Mexico City Bar, arrived at the small room where his client, Theodora Lupa, was waiting. Theodora Lupa, who had been detained for almost a week, looked completely exhausted. The forty-year-old foreigner was much more accustomed to social events than to the humid cells of Mexican prisons.

- Well?" she asked with feverish impatience.

- I'm sorry," the lawyer apologized, "but my request for release has been denied and your case will not be reviewed for at least 10 days.

- 10 days!" she panicked.

This was turning into a frenzy. The art dealer had specialized over the years in selling pieces of Aztec origin to wealthy collectors in the Lilleland region, and she had to admit that she often had to agree to work with traffickers. Having Mexican origins through her grandfather and also the dual nationality she had acquired to justify her frequent travels, she had thus managed to form a network parallel to the official channels and totally illegal, but which allowed her to obtain rare pieces and finance her lifestyle since her divorce. Who would have thought that, with the experience she had gained over the years, her latest deal could turn into such a fiasco. Yet it seemed to be the most lucrative deal she had ever done. A wealthy collector had asked her for a piece that was so rare and wanted so badly that he was willing to pay a sum that made her head spin. He had even paid a deposit that alone was worth as much as the amount she had received for her two previous imports. However, he also wanted it done quickly and she had had to travel in person to Mexico City to pick up the piece and it was there that things had escalated. She had been arrested by the local police when she had bought the coin and was now in jail for stealing a rare item.

Jail was horrible. The women she was with were all bullies and she had already escaped two attempts on her life despite her lawyer getting her a special regime that isolated her from others most of the time. Clearly, being European made her a prime target. As long as she maintained her special status, she was able to survive, but what would happen when she found herself mixed in with the other prisoners?

- What about the heart of the matter? she asked as soon as she got over her disappointment.

- 'That's not good,' Leo replied. The evidence is heavy. They have the record of the transaction and the testimony of the man who sold you the talisman. It's a piece of unique historical value according to experts, and our country has embarked on a policy of merciless warfare against looters of archaeological sites. Worst of all, they will use your dual nationality to claim that you are Mexican and thus thwart any attempt by your country of origin to repatriate you.

Theodora knotted her hands on the table, everything was going from bad to worse.

- What exactly am I risking?

- Through your seller, they think they can prove that you have been trafficking for years and they want an exemplary sentence. That could be anywhere from 20 to 30 years.

- 30 years?!? But that's worse than murder!!! This is absurd.

***

- I told you that a new law has been passed to mercilessly punish traffickers in archaeological pieces and you could be the victim.

- My God, I wouldn't last 30 days in that prison.

Leo Campo sighed.

- I understand, and I don't know how long I can continue with your preferential treatment.

He thought for a second and then looked back as if afraid their conversation might be overheard. Finally he leaned toward her.

- 'There might be a solution,' he murmured, 'but normally I wouldn't tell you about it because it's totally illegal.

- 'A solution,' Theodora said excitedly, leaning towards him.

- 'Yes,' said Leo, indicating that she had to be discreet. It's very complicated and risky, but it might work. You would have to confess to a crime committed in your own country, and a judge would request your extradition.

Theodora looked doubtful, not understanding anything at all.

- My country doesn't want to be mad at your country, and if they're mad at you it's because you have Mexican nationality, but if they were certain that your country's jurisdiction is looking for you for a crime at least as serious as the one they want to try you for, they wouldn't object to you being tried in your country for both crimes. Then an excellent lawyer could bury both cases.

- A crime for which I would face 30 years but would have to confess to at least one murder.

- Not necessarily a scam would be enough if it is on a large scale. It's not a question of punishment but the scale of the crime. The hard part is not so much finding a crime as it is finding a judge who is naive and motivated enough to ask for your extradition.... Unless he doesn't know you.

- I don't understand.

- As you may have guessed, I studied this case because I sensed that you would be in great difficulty. I discovered that by an incredible stroke of luck a very influential judge from your home region was vacationing in our country, his name is de Saint Servier. Do you know him?

- De Saint Servier? Theodora repeated.

Yes, she knew this fat, stiff man and, to tell the truth, she despised him. He was one of the bigwigs of the conservative party, while she herself had long been a member of the center-left party, his main opponent. She had even been elected while he was being nominated as the worst president the region had ever known, in her personal opinion. She had openly opposed him at the time and never failed to show her contempt whenever they crossed paths. Knowing this, why would he agree to help her?

- I know him, but he will never help me, she admitted.

- Yet he agreed to come see you in two days, Leo said.

She gave him an accusing look. She had made the decision to contact de Saint Servier without his permission.

- 'If you don't want his help, just tell him,' Leo decreed, not caring about her procrastination.

***

It was while returning to her cell that Theodora learned that her preferential treatment would end the next day and was forced to join a cell already occupied by five other women who stared at her as soon as they saw her. One of them, a fat, half-toothed matron, approached her as soon as the guards had left.

- 'You have beautiful fair skin,' she complimented her, running her hand over her cheek.

Theodora reflexively pushed the dirty hand away and the woman's face turned dark.

- The white woman thinks she's a queen," she snarled. She thinks she will be served tea.

The other women burst out laughing and Theodora didn't know what to say. Suddenly the woman pulled out an object and showed it to her. Theodora only managed to avoid having her throat slashed by the improvised knife, but it stuck in her wrist, which she had put on protectively. She cried out in pain as the matron lunged at her, trying to pull the weapon from her wound. The guards came running in and opened the cell. She was immediately taken to the infirmary and spent the day there before her meeting with de Saint Servier.

***

Judge de Saint Servier appeared strangely different to her. The almost senile old man looked almost younger and smarter, but Theodora attributed this to his imprisonment. Hanging out with the dregs of society for too long must have made any normal person look better than they actually were.

Immediately he noticed the large bandage on her arm and gave her an understanding smile.

- My poor Theodora, I am sorry for your plight. The rascals who rot in these prisons must not be soft.

She had certainly not lost her sense of understatement.

- Did Master Campo explain the situation to you?

- Yes, and he was very specific. He's a very smart lawyer to come up with such an idea, but he must also be a little crazy to propose such a thing to a man like me, especially considering our relationship so far.

- You're not going to help me.

- I never said that. I might, I happen to have a much better solution, I'm currently investigating the Blenon case. You do, I think. You used to be a great friend of Amandine Blenon's but you haven't talked to her since her husband ruined himself in this affair.

It wasn't that simple. Compromising with a woman linked to a crook would have ruined her political career and it was on the advice of her party chairman who had distanced himself from Amandine despite their friendship of many years.

- In short, it remains a very dark case and I am still looking for witnesses to shed light on it. I would only need to justify that you are one to get your extradition. You would also be protected from any prosecution during the time of the investigation, which could take years and even lead us to the statute of limitations on this obscure traffic case.

Theodora's heart stopped beating because it all seemed too good. She could regain her freedom.

- However," the judge continued, "if I do this for you, you will obviously have to pay the price.

- Whatever you want," she said, all too happy to escape the death this cursed Mexican prison had promised her. I'll give you all the information about my party, I'll be a defector, I'll even stay in the party and I'll tell you about their strategies.

She was ready to betray her best friends to save her life, but the judge only smiled wryly.

- As if I care, my dear. I've been manipulating your party for years into thinking they're a real opposition to us, when they're nothing but a bunch of spineless puppets who've never made me afraid.

- But then what do you want? I'm not rich enough to buy you, I know.

- But you, simply my dear. I want you. I want you at my beck and call, totally docile to my every desire.

For a second she thought he was joking, or worse, that he was doing it just to torture her, but he remained perfectly calm and she understood that he was totally serious.

- You can't expect me to accept this. I'm still Theodora Lupa and...

- And your days are numbered, my dear," de Saint Servier interrupted her. 'With your high-class habits, you will make a fortune in this prison. I've seen that you've already tasted the pleasures of community life, and believe me, it won't get any better. I know from my work what it's like in our country's prisons, so I can't even imagine what it's like in this one. You poor fool, if it were up to me, you could rot there, but it just so happens that I have promised you to a friend. He already has Amandine and would like to get the pair back together, but if you refuse, I'll be able to find another pretentious bourgeois to please him.

She stared stupidly at Saint Servier, unable to grasp the meaning of the words he was saying, so unreal did they seem to her. The judge understood her reaction perfectly and simply shrugged his shoulders like a child tired of an old toy. Then he stood up and walked briskly to the exit door. He tapped to open the door and she saw all her hopes for survival disappear with him. Despair took hold of her and he dictated the words that came out of her mouth.

- Don't go away! I'll give you anything you want, but don't go!

De Saint Servier turned around with a look of victory on his face. He signaled to the guard that he wasn't finished and returned to her.

- So we'll finally get along.

CHAPTER 7

She surrendered to him on everything. He made her sign many documents. In some of them she admitted false involvement in Blenon's scams and agreed to be extradited to her country. In others, however, she sold her entire property for a pittance to one David Angel, whom she didn't even know. The worst was when she gave up her original nationality and kept only her Mexican nationality.

She was about to find herself an immigrant in her own country, and it took her some time to understand the purpose of the maneuver: de Saint Servier became her only defense against an express return to Mexico. As a Mexican, she no longer had the same rights, and if he took away her status as a witness in the Blenon case, she would only be home for a few days before finding herself exactly where she was at the moment. She found herself a prisoner of her former political enemy.

However, in that moment, she saw only the fact that he kept his promise. De Saint Servier was a much more efficient man than she thought and the Mexican justice system bent to his will in record time and she was put on a plane under good security. The most terrifying thing was that she ran into de Saint Servier who was on the same flight as her. He was accompanied by a young blonde girl in her twenties who seemed distracted and realized she wasn't the first to fall into his clutches.

***

The flight seemed awfully long, so much so that his mind was haunted by the image of this girl obediently following de Saint Servier and the fear of one day becoming like her. When the plane landed, the Mexican police handed her over to their local counterparts and she was taken to court where she was held for a day. The next day she saw de Saint Servier again, who had reassumed his role as a judge.

- 'As I told you in our previous meeting, Madame Lupa,' he lied, 'you are now a protected witness and I will question you in due course. I am revoking your arrest warrant; you are free.

Her lawyer, a public defender since she could no longer afford to pay a high-priced lawyer, took her back to her apartment, which now belonged to a stranger. She went home and, exhausted, fell asleep fully clothed.

***

She was awakened hours later by someone knocking on her door. She looked through the door and saw the imposing mass of a black giant and recognized de Saint Servier's African driver. Her blood ran cold and she locked the door, but the man continued to pound on the door and then suddenly became angry and threw increasingly powerful punches to the point that the door opened. Subjected to such treatment, the lock eventually gave way. Pushed backwards, Theodora screamed, she never thought the man would be so strong.

- Get out or I'll call the police, she shouted.

But the man said nothing and, of course, did not leave. He walked over to her and put his strong hands around her neck. She struggled to resist and wanted to scream for help again, but the air was already running out and she sank into unconsciousness, convinced that she was living her last moments.

***

Theodora woke up, however, but she was no longer at home, but in the living room of a huge apartment she did not know. It took her a few moments to fully recover her senses and that's when she saw her. She was unmistakably the girl she had seen in de Saint Servier's presence. She was kneeling before her completely naked, her eyes downcast. This sight so overwhelmed her that she did not even notice the man who was sitting next to this poor soul.

- Our guest is finally awake, Madeleine," said de Saint Servier.

Hearing the judge's voice surely brought her out of her semi-conscious state. He was sitting on a red couch right next to the girl, his hand running through her hair. Theodora immediately had the image of an owner petting his dog and her heart sank.

- My driver explained your behavior to me, my dear, and I am disappointed. Especially since your new landlord will have to call a locksmith to fix your door. This is inexcusable.

- What did you expect? For me to obey you?

- But you have no choice. Have you already forgotten your friends from the prison in Mexico City?

He stood up abruptly and the young woman he had called Madeleine shook herself with her whole body to approach

Theodora. Still weak, the latter did not have the strength to get up and he took her by the arm.

- If so, I can offer you an internship in one of our most select prisons, just to give you a little refresher course, and if that's not enough, I'll offer you a free trip to the land of Mexico. I've made a bet with friends that you won't survive for more than two days, and I hate to lose a bet.

Her arm turned blue under his grip and she couldn't suppress a sob. She'd never realized how tough this man, whom she'd always thought of as a second-rate politician, was.

He challenged the flap of the robe he wore and presented her with his powerful member.

- Suck it, Paquita! he ordered.

Defeated, she took the old man's sex into her mouth.

***

The judge had finally overcome the resistance of this proud slut. It had taken him a long time and a lot of effort but at least it had been done and now Angel would get what he wanted and be able to enjoy little Blenon as planned. At the moment though, all he could think about was this bourgeois woman's active mouth on his sex and he had to admit she was talented. Although his arousal hadn't been extreme at first, he now felt totally overwhelmed with desire. Theodora knew how to use her tongue and even used her hand in hopes of bringing him to orgasm quickly but he was too used to this little game to let it get to him. Once he was well warmed up, he pushed her violently back against the couch, she screamed in surprise but showed no sign of resistance. He smiled, pleased with her newfound docility. He had obviously understood that it was not in her interest to challenge him. He bent down to her level and looked into her eyes to read the signs of her submission. At the same time, his hands rested on her blouse and, without mercy, he tore it off, revealing her breasts. By reflex, she wanted to hide her now revealed breasts but he spread her arms and pressed himself against her, rubbing his chest against hers. Their faces made contact and she wanted to pull away again but he forced her to look at him and kiss him. He inserted his tongue into her mouth, hungrily searching for a tongue that was trying to escape hers. Gradually he forced her to lie on her back and his hands went down to her pants and began to undo her zipper. As he began to remove his pants, she lifted her buttocks almost by reflex to make the task easier. Once free of these pants, he found himself installed between her thighs and observed for a moment her crotch which only a small white silk panty still protected from his assaults. With a quick movement, he tore them off and plunged his head towards her clit which he began to titillate. He wanted to make her come and with his usual skill combined with this woman's responsive body, he achieved that goal at a speed that almost surprised him. When he looked up, his mouth drenched in her powder, he read the shame on her face at the orgasm he had just given her; she was ready for the kill.

He thrust into her violently and she almost gave in under the shock of his penetration. Then he lay on top of her and began to come and go as he kissed her hungrily. Now totally focused on his pleasure, he sped up the pace without caring about the cries of the woman who was trapped in his hands. Theodora's ordeal lasted for many minutes, then suddenly he came inside her and her screams increased as she realized this horrible reality.

Then he stood up, leaving her to her tears. He grabbed Madeleine, who had remained obediently kneeling where he had left her, and forced her to clean his cock, which was dirty with his cum and

Theodora's wetness. Now conditioned by long weeks with him, the girl was unfailingly obedient in these debasing tasks.

The judge turned back to Theodora, who remained curled up on the couch.

- For a first time, it was more than satisfactory, he thought. Now you will go home but of course you will remain at my complete disposal. Don't ever forget that you belong to me.

Theodora didn't answer. She simply straightened up, trying to recover an illusion of dignity. She put her pants back on and closed the tattered blouse over her bare chest. She knew she was making a pitiful spectacle, but she had only one idea: get out of this place. She stood up and headed for the door. Just as she had almost reached it, de Saint Servier's voice called to her.

- I forgot, my dear. A friend of mine is throwing a little party and he absolutely wants us to attend...both of us.

Once again she remained silent but had to make an enormous effort to hold back more sobs; tonight was only the beginning.

CHAPTER 8

Amandine Blenon now understood the meaning of the word "loneliness" from the last few days when she had been forced to empty herself. First she had had to throw out her sister's family, and that without mercy, to comply with Angel's orders. The breakup with Laurine, her younger sister, had been terrible. She was driving them apart, even though they had given her unconditional support during the trials she had had to endure because of her husband's greed and cowardice.

Of course, she hadn't been able to reveal to them that she was doing all this to preserve them; Angel had even threatened to blackmail Laurine if she ever broke her silence. So she had had to let them go, knowing that they would never forgive her.

But that wasn't the worst part: the worst part came with Maria's departure. Her youngest daughter had cried and then screamed, totally refusing to be separated from her mother and sister so soon after losing her father. Amandine's mother's heart had been permanently broken when she had abandoned her daughter in her parents' home. They had not blamed her, but she had felt the weight of their accusing looks as she walked back to her car, gathering all her strength to resist the urge to go back and keep her daughter close.

During those awful days, the only support she could count on was Laura but she hadn't felt so distant from her older daughter since the depraved evening Angel had put them through. Amandine could not accept the ease with which the latter had submitted to their torturer nor the fact that she had agreed to help him break her mother's resistance.

But the most terrible thing for Amandine was that these painful days were only the prelude to her new life.

* * *

Two days before Angel's official move into their home, a strange man arrived on his own. He told them that his name was Jasper and that he was in charge of directing the changes in the house that was already no longer theirs. So the second floor of the villa was completely renovated in record time by several teams of workers. Amandine and Laura had to sleep in the living room and were horrified to discover that three of the four bedrooms had been changed.

Each room had been fitted with a security door that could no longer be locked from the inside, but had a centrally controlled locking system like in prisons. And that was what this place would be to them. Inside the rooms, unlike the rest of the house, all the wallpaper had been removed, leaving only the walls painted a dull gray. There was only a large double bed, a toilet and, worst of all, a wide-angle camera in the upper right corner. The impression of imprisonment was further reinforced.

- Of course, not all installations are finished, Jasper said in his falsetto voice. The video network will take weeks to be operational, but Mr. Angel is very demanding and wanted this initial work completed by tonight.

Amandine wanted to wipe the smile off his face as she said this, but she merely clenched her fists as she made her way to the last room, the one that had been hers and her husband's; the contrast was striking. Their large bed had been replaced by an equally large but much more lavish and gilded one. On the wall were paintings by great masters and in front of the bed was a console with several small screens, and it didn't take a genius to figure out that this was where the images from the house's cameras converged when they were on. Amandine knew immediately that she was in Angel's room.

Jasper seemed pleased with the work of the workers and told them he would be back in a few days to oversee further work. Before leaving mid-afternoon, he gave them a large cardboard box and told them to wait until Angel arrived before opening it.

***

Angel arrived as the sun was setting. He didn't need to ring the doorbell, and they understood that he had already done everything necessary to let everyone know that he was the new owner of the place and that it wouldn't be long before their ruin would be known throughout the city. Of course, he already had the key to the front door and it was the sound of the door slamming that alerted them to his arrival.

When they arrived in the great hall from the kitchen for one and from upstairs for the other, they found him in the hall by the fireplace. He had built a fire and was waiting for them, displaying the arrogance that defined him in Amandine's eyes. He sat down on one of the couches in the center of the room, indicating, if it was necessary to specify, his new status. He nodded and ordered them to sit across from him. Amandine wanted to sit down but Angel's dark gaze prevented her from doing so.

- I see you brought my little gift," she said, pointing to the box left by Jasper that Laura had put on the coffee table. Amandine, open it!

After a moment of hesitation, she bent down to open the box. Then she discovered two transparent covers that protected some very unusual clothes. Amandine easily discerned a light apron, shiny shoes, and a small hat; servant's clothing that couldn't have been smaller.

- 'These are your new work clothes,' Angel explained. 'Since you have become my slaves, it is only natural that you wear them. Wear them!

With a lump in her throat, Amandine watched her daughter, still submissive as ever to this monster, begin to undress. Eventually she did the same, removing her clothes to keep only her underwear, but the voice of her tormentor immediately rang out.

- What did I say? I didn't want any more underwear.

Strangely, she felt like a child caught in the act when she realized that Laura was completely naked, but she refused to accept the idea that she would have to wear this indecent attire without any clothes to protect her private parts. He could feel Angel's gaze on her and remembered the violence he was capable of when resisted. He moved to get up and she hurried to remove her bra. He sat back down, clearly pleased with the fear he had instilled in her. When they were both naked, he turned his head toward the covers. Laura grabbed the one with her name on it and ripped off the plastic to get her clothes out. As always, Amandine hesitated for a moment, but eventually followed her daughter's lead.

Thus dressed, she felt horribly exposed. The back of her apron was reduced to the waistband needed to hold it in place, so she ended up with her back and, more importantly, her butt bare. The front wasn't much better. Very short, it barely protected her groin and her breasts, though not very developed, were barely concealed. Laura's, on the other hand, was oppressed and emerged at the sides. Angel seemed to enjoy this sight. She then stood up and gathered their clothes and walked over to the fireplace. Under their stunned eyes, he threw them into the fire to which he added a small accelerator to make sure they burned well.

- You won't need them anymore. These will be your only clothes. As you may have noticed, the workers removed all the clothes in your closets.

This was the answer to the question Amandine had asked herself after spending half the afternoon searching for her clothes in the closets upstairs. Now her designer clothes were about to be worn by the wives of the workers who had raided the closets in her house.

Angel returned to his seat, sat down and turned his head toward Laura.

- Come here!

Obedient as ever, the girl stepped forward and knelt before him. As he had done a week before, he felt with pleasure her opulent breasts through the miserable protection of her apron.

- Amandine, there is something else in the box, another gift for you. Take it!

Anxiously, she rummaged through the box and pulled out a small black plastic bat that she recognized immediately. It was a dildo. She was reassured to see that it wasn't a huge diameter, but she also realized that it wasn't a conventional dildo since it had a strap-on. She realized that it was meant to be worn all the time.

- On our first night, I was frustrated," Angel recalled. I wasn't able to do a procedure I wanted to do...because of you.

It didn't take her long to realize what she was talking about: his sodomy. She stiffened and dropped the dildo in terror.

- I think you get the idea. This dildo is designed to widen your little ring so I won't have trouble fucking you next time. It has a flat bottom, so all you have to do is put it on the table and impale yourself on it.

- Never! He shouted. Not like this!

Angel turned to Laura, smiling at her, and a second later he punched her in the stomach, taking her breath away. The girl doubled over, her eyes filled with tears. Angel turned back to Amandine, her treacherous smile still on her face.

- It's your choice...

And without finishing the sentence, she delivered a second blow to the girl who had just straightened up, knocking her to the ground. Without mercy, Angel forced her up by pulling her by the ponytail. She was panting in pain and her still teenage eyes showed nothing but terror. She closed her fist.

- Stop!" shouted her mother. Stop, I will...I will.

Angel unclenched his fist but didn't let go of Laura's ponytail. Slowly, reluctantly, Amandine bent down to pick up the dildo and placed it on the coffee table as he had indicated. As she touched it, she noticed that it was slipping. It had been lubricated and that reassured her a little. Aware that this monster who took as much pleasure in raping her as he did in making her suffer would want to witness her torment completely, she turned to him and began to lower herself onto the taut plastic window. The cold contact of the plastic caused a reflex reaction and her anal sphincter muscles made contact to resist this unnatural penetration. She could not relax but forced herself to continue her act in spite of everything and the first few inches marked the beginning of her suffering. She gritted her teeth to avoid giving this man she hated the pleasure of hearing her scream but she felt tears of sweat beading on her temples as she pushed this artificial member into her bowels.

In front of her, Angel had unbuttoned his pants and led his daughter's head to his member. Despite the abuse he had inflicted on her, Laura continued to slavishly obey this monster; she swallowed his member in her mouth without blinking.

However, Amandine was far from these considerations, so much so that the pain caused by the rigid object she was forced to insert into her anal cavity made her live in martyrdom. It took all her willpower not to scream but she had to face the reality, she would never have the strength to complete the operation and, when she had pushed it in almost halfway, she could no longer find the resources to go any further.

At that moment, he saw that sadistic smile on Angel's face that he knew all too well. He pushed Laura's head back mercilessly and stood up to move closer to her. He gently ran his hand through her hair, keeping that smile that to others might have seemed reassuring. Then, suddenly, she put her hands on Amandine's shoulders and pushed violently so that the dildo entered her completely with a loud snap. The cold touch of the table on her buttocks was the last of the sensations compared to the wave of pain that swept over her like a tide and, despite all her determination, she couldn't help but scream.

Without seeming to care about her screams, Angel tightened the straps of the dildo around her belly to make sure it remained perfectly secured in her anus even if she had to move. Totally in shock, Amandine let herself be made like a doll.

At that moment, a ringing sounded and it took Amandine, whose mind was dominated by pain, several seconds to recognize the call on the intercom.

- One of our guests has just arrived," Angel explained simply. Laura will open the door for them!

Guests? A real panic seized the bourgeois woman. This monster had not only planned to humiliate them and make them suffer, but he had brought people to witness the pathetic spectacle of his degradation.

However, she quickly forgot her apprehensions when Angel grabbed her by the hair, pulling her with him. A new wave of pain emanated from her insides and she totally abandoned all dignity to let her suffering speak for itself: she cried out with every step. He sat back down on the couch he had occupied earlier and forced her to kneel, her buttocks erect, to take the role abandoned by her daughter.

CHAPTER 9

The guest was indeed a guest. Christine had surrendered to her rapist's blackmail and it was with a lump in her throat that she drove her car to the Blenon mansion. Then she had an incongruous thought: she thought of her father. He had been in business with Jerome Blenon for a long time and must have visited this place many times. Yet he did not remember this man or his family.

That was because the association between the two men had been going on for about ten years when she was just a young woman in her twenties. Her father, as an authoritarian patriarch, had kept her away from the region by prohibiting her from studying at the nearby university in Fortlud. She had never understood the reasons behind her father's decision, other than the fact that he felt Lilleland and its region had become dangerous for her.

When he finally allowed her to return, he simply told her that 'her brother had finally done his duty' without going into details. She had thus regained her place in the small regional microcosm, but Blenon was already no longer part of her father's connections. Her father was now dead and she had never heard of Blenon before the dark business deal in which he had swallowed her entire fortune and that of several other notables... before tonight.

She parked in the small parking lot in front of the mansion and saw that there was only one other car. She walked to the front door and reached for the doorbell with a trembling hand, but at the last moment her strength failed her. She wanted to turn back, but the choice was lost, for the door opened and she found herself facing a young girl in her early twenties, whose attire put an end to all her illusions. She wore only a simple white apron, very tight at the waist, which showed off her large breasts and left her legs completely bare.

- 'The master is waiting for you,' said the girl, who must have been barely of age, and turned to tell him to come in after her.

Christine noticed almost without surprise that this indecent attire left her buttocks completely bare and swallowed her saliva before she found the strength to enter this house where she already knew she would suffer martyrdom.

She crossed a small hallway into a large, well-decorated living room and again witnessed a scene that terrified her. The man who had raped her was sitting on a couch and between his legs was another woman giving him oral sex. In this position, Christine could not see her clothing but could easily guess that she was dressed in the same way as the young woman who had taken her in, but that was not what shocked her the most. In this position, felix's buttocks were prominent and Christine easily distinguished the black circle between the two round globes: she had been sodomized with a dildo. A door in Christine's mind opened and she wanted to run away from this hellish place. However, she remained totally still, staring at this stranger who with one decision could destroy her whole life.

- Welcome my dear," said the man and Christine finally remembered that her name was Angel. I'm glad you came. Come on Laura, release our guest!

The girl jumped as if she had been slapped and came towards her.

- Your jacket, please, ma'am....

- Your jacket! Angel growled, "What an idiot. Do you think I came for tea? She's here to be fucked just like you so undress her!

The girl, Laura, stiffened and hurried to obey as if she desperately wanted to please the man. Christine would not deny herself and pushed her away without violence to unbutton her blouse.

- Am I speaking Czech or what? Angel then became angry. I ordered Laura to do it, not you, so let her do it!

Without waiting for her reaction, Laura put her hands under her armpits and started to undo the last buttons of her blouse. Taken aback, Christine remained unresponsive. She could feel the girl's ample breasts pressing against her back and her breath against her neck as she pushed the blouse aside. Their two bare skins made contact and, against her will, her breathing quickened.

As if on purpose, Laura let her hands slide over her body before sliding the hooks of her bra and Christine realized that this little game was wanted by Angel. He was toying with her by leaving her in the hands of this little girl barely younger than Natacha hoping to reproduce the same shameful emotion that had made her fall into his clutches.

The horrible thing was that it worked. She felt herself leave as the young adult's hands unfastened the waistband of her pants. She was already a disjointed puppet and cursed herself for her weakness, knowing she was sinking even deeper. Pressing herself against her willingly, Laura reached down to remove her pants. Almost impatiently, she lifted one leg and then the other to make it easier for him. Her hands slid up his legs causing shivers of excitement. Laura's hands rested on the sides of her panties but did not pull them down.

They plunged into her intimacy. This was the coup de grace, Christine let out a moan of pleasure as if in anticipation and memories of her embrace with Natasha came flooding back. She found the energy to pull herself away from the damn baby and end the trap, and removed her panties herself as quickly as she could. As she straightened up, she caught Angel's eye, and her toothy smile indicated that she had gotten exactly what she wanted.

- Did you get what I wanted?" she asked as she placed her hand on the woman who was tending to her sex to adjust her pace to her liking.

Ashamed, he turned his head to the briefcase he had brought with him, which lay next to his clothes. Laura brought it to him without her having to say anything. She took it and, with a heavy heart, opened it and placed its contents on the small glass table in front of her.

- Sit down," Angel ordered her as she straightened up.

He pushed her aside, making her moan in pain, and Christine realized that the instrument he had inserted into her anal orifice was the cause. Angel looked at the files he had brought with him and then at her.

- 'You're kidding me, aren't you?

- Not at all," she stammered. 'I kept my promise, these are the files of the girls we are responsible for....

- I also wanted the reports of some of my colleagues," he interrupted her. Where are they?

- No! Not that one!

He shook his head as if tired of saying the same thing over and over again and then with an immediacy that left her without reaction, he stood up, closed the distance between them and slapped her twice with such violence that she was left with a terrible feeling of heat for many minutes. Since he had raped her at her workplace, she knew he was a brutal man, but this was like a reminder. He could hurt her both physically and emotionally. He grabbed her by the wrist and twisted it until she screamed.

- I want those files," he spat in her face, squeezing even harder, and suddenly he was the only thing in the world she considered. 'I want them before two days when I destroy you and every member of your family without exception!

- You will have them! Christine cried and at this point had only one thought in her mind, make him leave.

He loosened his grip but didn't release her and looked into her eyes like a predator and she realized she would give him what he wanted if he wanted to save what he could. She smiled again, fully aware that she had achieved the goal she was looking for, and returned to her seat. He grabbed the blonde woman by the ears and forced her to resume her fellatio. Once again she moaned in pain but complied.

He ordered Laura to bring him a glass of water. Still in shock, she drank with pleasure. He smiled softly and spoke again.

- Although I'm a little disappointed with what you brought me, I could be satisfied for now and give you a small reward as well. Laura.

He turned to the girl and motioned for her to come and sit beside her. She shuddered with apprehension when she felt the presence of this desirable and almost naked girl next to her again. Laura turned back to Angel, obviously awaiting instructions. He merely nodded and she moved even closer, wanting to pull back but her head began to spin and she realized that he had drugged her again. She fell backwards and found herself helpless. Laura was able to lie on top of her, his young round body rubbed against hers without her being able to resist him because of the softness of the couch they were sitting on. The girl slid her lips over his, inserting her tongue into his mouth. When his left hand began to knead her right breast, she was again invaded by this hellish mess that she had rejected with her whole being and it was when Laura's right hand invaded her intimacy that she began to return his unnatural kiss. Then she lost herself in this unhealthy embrace, her hands ventured through the girl's apron, playing on her very developed nipples and then she wanted to taste them in her mouth and smell her pussy. She felt like a bitch in heat and she didn't care that her partner was a child barely of age; all that mattered was her shape and the pleasure she was bringing him at that moment.

She was brought out of this state by a ringing bell.

- 'Here are our other guests,' Angel announced simply, clearly pleased. I feel sorry for you Christine, but your little friend will have business elsewhere.

* * *

Laura broke away from the furious lesbian and readjusted her dress. Walking to the front door she saw a new face of a woman she knew. She was a friend of her mother's and wondered if she should spend the evening kissing other women. He opened the door and waited in the doorway for the doorbell to ring. The waiting time was not as long as it was for the previous guest and she opened the door immediately. She was relieved to see that it was indeed a couple and a little less relieved to realize the age of the man, who had to be over 60. The latter went forward to his companion.

- Laura", he said, looking at her with a concupiscent air that hid nothing of his intentions. I am so happy to meet you. If you only knew how long I have waited.

She did not know this man, but he seemed to know her. She followed the instructions imposed by her master and was polite.

- Pleased to meet you, sir. If you would like to follow me.

- But with pleasure," the old man replied.

She turned to show him the way and at that moment he put his hand on her bare buttocks. She was frightened but knew she could not react. He had all the rights and she had none. So they arrived in the living room and she witnessed for the second time the grotesque close-up of her mother's buttocks being squeezed with a dildo. The old man laughed and the woman with him sobbed in horror.

- My dear judge," said the master. What a pleasure to have you here, plus you brought me a wonderful gift: Theodora Lupa.

Her mother stopped her fellatio at the mention of this name and wanted to turn her head, but the master put his hands on the back of her head to make her understand that this was out of the question and she gave up and returned to her previous occupation. At that moment the old man's hand went even further into the cleft of her buttocks and she tensed and he turned to face her. She shuddered when she realized what was waiting for her, she was going to end up in bed with him.

- 'I know you are impatient, my friend,' said the master. I suggest you take advantage of one of the rooms upstairs.

- Excellent," replied the old man that the master had appointed only the judge. I will leave Theodora as pawn as planned.

- Laura", ordered the master, "lead our guest!

Obediently, she turned and headed for the stairs. She led the judge to the room that was once hers and invited him in. The judge watched her with interest and seemed to appreciate the decor, especially the camera. He turned to her and drew her to him for a kiss. The old man's tongue in her mouth made her want to vomit far more than the woman she had sought out moments before. His hand had already gone around her body and untied the knot in her apron belt. He was rubbing himself against her like an animal and she could feel the strength of his erection. He removed her apron before making her lie on her back, legs open. She remembered her master's exploration of her intimacy a week earlier but felt no arousal at the idea of feeling this old man's tongue plunging into her slit.

However, he didn't care and spread her labia to plunge his tongue into her genital opening and then began to play with her clit. For the first time in her life, a man's tongue (not a teenager's) was playing with her pleasure. An unknown wave swept over her quickly against her will and she let herself be carried away without any remorse forgetting the nature of the one who was bringing her this ecstasy. Quickly, the judge withdrew his tongue from her vagina, which was drenched with abundant powder, he seemed satisfied.

- You're a real little slut just like Angel promised me," he said. Nothing like the little slut sharing my life. That's fine and we'll spice it up.

He reached into his pocket and pulled out a pair of handcuffs. She had often heard of this type of play but had never played it and in her excited state she felt ready to give in to all the whims of this lecherous old man. He turned her around and pushed her back towards the bedpost. He trapped her hands between the frames so that she could not move and forced her forward. She was now doggy style and he plunged his hand into her vaginal cavity, which was still profusely wet. She was so aroused that this simple gesture was enough to make her react.

However, he did not linger and, to her horror, immediately pulled out his wet fingers and plunged them into her now fully exposed anus. She then realized the purpose of the maneuver and wanted to escape but she was trapped in the bedpost and he grabbed her hips to force her to stay in place. She was trapped and began to scream as soon as she felt the tip of his glans press against her anal orifice.

She had not reacted when she had witnessed her mother's two sodomies, but now she understood the hell she had been and was still being subjected to. The judge had no mercy, he pushed his member into her still virgin cavity with unfailing firmness taking advantage of her position and she knew he would not stop until he had penetrated her completely.

She abandoned all dignity and screamed as much as she could as the sex progressed. She thought her ordeal was over when she felt the contact of his purse against her buttocks, but she was wrong, because he began to piston her and she reached a new level of suffering. She clung to the back of the bed as he moved in and out (a few inches but enough to make her life a living hell on earth) inside her. He had slumped onto his back and was groping her breasts, going back and forth with the ledge at the same time and she could feel his breath on her neck. She screamed even louder!

CHAPTER 10

Laura's screams echoed through the living room and the three women present tensed.

- 'Laura is discovering new pleasures,' sneered Angel as he grabbed Amandine's face to get a better look at the tears streaming down her face.

He rudely pushed her away, causing her to stand up. She screamed again from the pain emanating from her invaded anus. He forced her to sit up and her pain intensified. With a glance, he ordered Christine closer. Now complacent, the educator moved closer and thrust his head into Laura's mother. Still under the influence of the girl's excitement and the drug, she did not hesitate to give a piece to her mother. For Amandine it was the beginning of a new horror, between the pain in her anus and an unnatural pleasure in her pussy but she was so weakened that she had no strength to resist. Angel could then focus on the last of her victims.

Theodora was left standing, totally petrified by the obscene spectacle she was forced to witness. Perhaps she had convinced herself that by being as discreet as possible, she would eventually be forgotten. Bad luck, with Angel this was not likely.

He walked over to her and placed his hands on the heart-shaped patch she was wearing. He slid his hands behind her back to loosen the two flaps.

- 'You know I've been waiting for this moment for a long time, Madame Lupa,' he explained, untying the two strips. 'Exactly since the day I discovered your ex-husband had defrauded my company.

She pulled the sides of her wrap, revealing the white satin bra chosen by the judge.

- You knew that your beautiful apartment was paid for in part with my money, and I'm certainly not a good Samaritan.

He pulled back the heart patch so that her arms were pulled back and her hands were trapped. He removed her bra and began kneading her breasts, smiling.

- Now everything will go back to normal because thanks to you I have become an unavoidable partner for Mr. Durant, your ex-husband, and he will find out how formidable I can be in this position. As for you, you will regret taking advantage of that ill-gotten money.

- I didn't," she whined, perhaps hoping to soften her tormentor.

But of course Angel didn't care about such considerations. He pushed her backwards and flipped her over onto one of the couches, legs up. He rolled up her skirt and ripped off her panties. He paused for a moment to enjoy Laura's screams, which dragged on and on, then threw himself on top of her. He penetrated her mercilessly, wallowing in her. She showed an impressive docility that proved the judge had already begun his training well. Excited to the max by Amandine's work and Christine's little lesbian games, he still failed to take full advantage of this superb woman and came inside her enjoying with pleasure the submissive expression she was showing.

He got up to find that Laura's screams had stopped. A few moments later, the judge came downstairs, naked, with an expression of joy on his face.

- The baby is resting," he said. It must be said that our little session did? surprised her.

They burst out laughing together and returned their attention to Christine and Amandine. Totally uninhibited, the teacher seemed to have forgotten them. She continued to lick the former mistress' pussy without bothering to totally expose her most intimate parts. With a gesture, Angel invited the judge to take advantage of the opportunity. Still green despite her first round with the Blenon girl, the latter didn't hesitate and immediately went behind Christine's back who realized her presence too late.

He froze between her loins, causing her to cry out in surprise. She then clung to Amandine as he made out with her doggy style. Angel approached in turn. The judge saw this and pulled Christine violently by the ponytail. She pulled away from Amandine, obviously unwillingly, and Angel was able to freeze in the woman's blonde pussy. Angel did not tire of humiliating this fabulous bourgeois, and as she enjoyed her body, she was already imagining the future abuse she would put her through. Amandine was now being penetrated by both orifices at the same time and began to scream louder as Angel took pleasure in her.

***

The evening finally came to an end. The two men were full and left the four women completely exhausted to go have one last drink in the kitchen. Judge admired the facilities of his friend's new residence. He particularly liked the video system.

- So tell me," Angel said. How are you doing with the last part of the contract?

- It's going well,' he replied. It will be my masterpiece, believe me. And our friends?

- They're doing well. Uron has taken over the Saturday Bear hotel and intends to make the most of it.

Ruining Saturday Bear, the region's biggest fortune, had been the club's masterstroke, though the judge had deemed it premature.

- As for Diaz, he plans to open a very special bar, but I don't know much about it.

- I'm sure we'll hear from them when they're ready. They won't want to be outdone on the big night.

***

The horrible night was finally over. Lying on one of the couches, Amandine was coming to her senses. Her anus continued to make her suffer a martyrdom but she accepted this pain; she had known worse. The judge of Saint Servier, who was investigating her husband's misdeeds, and Theodora, her former friend, had been the first to leave. The young woman who, to her shame, had given him pleasure, had to wait a little longer for Angel to allow her to dress. There was no doubt that she too was a victim of their suborner despite the fact that she had finally succumbed to the horrors he had forced upon her. She had left in the night and Amandine could swear she was in tears. She found herself alone with the man who now decided her fate.

For the umpteenth time, he forced her to get up and a new wave of pain surged through her. She screamed again and he smiled. He handed her some small keys.

- Go and free your daughter! he ordered.

Without a word, she headed for the stairs. Each step was an ordeal and she found some relic of her former dignity to grit her teeth and stop screaming. She arrived at her daughter's room and entered, apprehensive of what she would find.

Laura lay curled up on the bed, her arms trapped in the bedpost by the handcuffs. She was crying. In this position, a trickle of semen could be seen dripping between her buttocks.

Amandine approached her and placed a hand on her shoulder, causing her to jump and her crying increased. He whispered words of comfort in her ear before reaching for the handcuffs to unfasten them. Once her hands were free, Laura curled up even more into a fetal position. Amandine regained her maternal instincts and put her arms around her daughter. At that moment, the door closed and Amandine realized that they were condemned to share this one-bed cell. She put the horrible thought out of her mind for the moment and thought only of cheering up the only child left with her.

CHAPTER 11

- What's up?" came the judge's voice into the telephone receiver.

- For the moment, she's wisely staying home," Jerome replied a little sheepishly.

- This is not acceptable," said his interlocutor angrily. I have obligations and especially Madeleine is starting to feel lonely.

- But.

- I don't want any buts! I understand that you are not yet up to the task. I will intervene to help you but this is the last time. Don't forget that if you're not useful to me, I won't pay you the second part of the amount.

He cut the call without waiting and Jerome pitied himself inwardly. He had already spent all the money he had earned by delivering Madeleine to that old scoundrel, and he knew that he could not bear to do without this providential boon. He was furious with this damned bitch who was in danger of losing everything. It certainly wasn't as easy to trap Sarah Bonnet as it was with her older sister.

***

The weeks following Madeleine's disappearance were incredibly painful for Sarah. The girl had never gotten along with her parents, especially her mother, who had considered her almost a failure since she was forced to repeat her junior year of high school. Often their exchanges would turn stormy and it was only thanks to her older sister's diplomatic talents that they avoided the worst. Now she no longer had that saving grace, and her sister's escape had further accentuated her mother's inquisitive behavior. She felt even more spied on and had no freedom.

When she wasn't at school, she was confined to her parents' apartment and could only escape this oppressive world by telling dangerous lies.

That day, however, she had taken no chances and found herself in her room, alone. It was early evening and her parents had not yet returned from work. Every day, she had about an hour of peace before her father returned and inevitably questioned her to make sure she hadn't skipped school to 'go mess with the thugs'. She didn't want to think about it and was enjoying these moments of respite from a life that had become horribly painful.

She was pulled out of her thoughts by a tap on the front door. Startled, she got out of bed, crossed the living room of the small apartment and looked through the peephole to see a man in his fifties with a thin mustache and a bald head that she recognized immediately. It was the policeman who had arrived at their home more than two months ago and interviewed them all. So it was with a mixture of anxiety and hope that she opened the door.

The man gave her a smile that was meant to be reassuring, but unconsciously she stepped back in front of this man who was taller than her by a head.

- Hello, young lady," he said. I don't know if you remember me. I'm Superintendent Giroud, we've met....

- I remember," she interrupted him. My parents are not here.

- Oh, that's too bad. I came to talk to them about your sister.

- Did you find her?

- Found her?" repeated Giroud, as if the question hadn't even arisen.

***

He hesitated for a moment, as if considering his answer.

- 'Not yet,' he said finally, but Sarah got the impression he wasn't sincere. I've come to bring you some things we don't need anymore.

He handed her a small package. She remembered that he had searched her room for evidence but had no idea what she had taken with her besides the drugs. She took the package. Giroud then greeted her and left. He closed the door and returned to the living room. He wanted to put the package on the table but at the last moment he couldn't resist opening it. He found Madeleine's phone and, above all, a strange little notebook that he did not know. He opened it and flipped through it quickly to realize that it was some kind of diary. It was a shock because she had no idea her sister kept one. She immediately realized its importance, as it could help her understand what had driven her sister to crime. She then decided to hide the cop pass from her parents and keep the notebook to herself.

***

Reading Madeleine's journal shocked Sarah. Madeleine had written it precisely, one page for one day. Sometimes the page was almost blank and sometimes it was completely blackened by her writing. She had only recently started writing it in fact, as if a particular event had prompted her to put her innermost thoughts on paper. In the first few pages, Madeleine openly accused her mother of turning in Jerome, her boyfriend, and doing everything she could to keep them from being together. She then explained how he comforted and supported her through the difficult times.

Sarah did not know Jerome and avoided him like most of the young boys in the neighborhood, who were too superficial for her. She met a few boys, but they were just friends from school and nothing more. This was fine with her because she didn't want a clingy boyfriend who would try to spy on her like her parents already did. She spent several hours finding out her sister's state of mind until the horrible revelation, the latter confessed to buying drugs to escape the family home to live with Jerome. She closed the notebook in shock.

She had convinced herself of her sister's innocence, of the manipulation of this Jerome who could only be a good-for-nothing. Now she had to face the reality that Madeleine was indeed a criminal. It took her several minutes to work up the courage to reopen her notebook and begin reading her sister's writings again in hopes of finding some justification. She read quickly, anxiously, and finally arrived at the fateful moment when this commissioner would arrive at their home. During this time Madeleine wrote down her fear, insisting that she was sure that if her mother found out anything she would tell the police.

Sarah then thought about what the policeman had said when he arrived, "you called me ma'am." Of course, her mother had said that she had nothing to do with the raid, but Sarah couldn't help but feel that her denials lacked conviction.

Still, the newspaper hadn't delivered all of her surprises, the last of which was the biggest. It didn't stop with the day Madeleine ran away. She continued almost a month later. Madeleine then talked about a place where she was locked up: a kind of asylum where the police had taken her after her arrest. She never specified where this place was, but she continued to pour out her resentment toward her parents, whom she held responsible for her imprisonment.

The last page she wrote was dated three days ago, and Sarah realized that they had lied to her about not knowing where her sister was. She lay down on the bed and began to cry in anger. She stayed like that for a few moments and then decided to fight back. Finding his sister was the best way to thwart the plans of his parents, who always seemed to want to dominate their lives, but he needed help to do it and his friends weren't the right ones to do it. She took Madeleine's cell phone and searched the directory for the number she wanted.

***

Jerome sobbed in surprise when he saw Madeleine's phone number appear. He knew full well that his ex-girlfriend was now the judge's blow-up doll and that he no longer had access to her phone. He hesitated for a second but decided to answer it.

- Hello?" he said, waiting for the answer.

- Jerome?" asked a voice he immediately recognized with relief. I'm Sarah, Madeleine's sister. I'd like to meet you soon.

- What's going on?" she answered, imitating panic perfectly. Is it Madeleine? Have you heard anything? Has something happened to her?

- I want to see you," she insisted.

- I want to see you," he insisted. "All right. I can come to your school tomorrow morning if you want.

- Out the south gate at eleven.

He hung up. He'd shown an authoritarian streak that didn't surprise Jeremy. Since he had been trying to get close to this seventeen-year-old girl, he had been able to get a feel for her character and realize that she was very different from his sister. The other students at his high school had nicknamed her the princess because of her tough and sometimes haughty behavior. For two months, all his attempts to approach her had been bitter failures, and it had only taken one day for the judge to break the deadlock. Satisfied with this news, Jerome turned to the girl who shared his bed.

***

The next day, Jerome was present for his appointment. He had parked his car a reasonable distance away because he wanted to maintain his image as a discreet young man. Sarah arrived about ten minutes late. He adopted a worried expression and walked over to her.

- 'Let's not stay here,' he said with the same directive as always.

He realized that she was skipping school to see him and he was glad: she was starting to take risks.

- Let's go for a drink," he suggested, not wanting her to take all the initiative.

They sat down in the room of a small café quite far from the school. Sarah didn't want to risk being seen in his presence. Jeremy understood her reticence-he must have been considered the devil personified by his family since the fall of St. Magdalene-but he intended to do everything he could to break down her resistance. Discreetly, he detailed her: she undeniably resembled Magdalene but seemed strangely more mature.

Physically she appeared better proportioned with a slightly less developed chest but a much slimmer pelvis. She tied her hair back in a much more controlled ponytail than Madeleine, and Jerome thought she gave off a much more impressive sex appeal than her sister. However, his investigation of her had uncovered no current or previous boyfriends. He realized that this was what had attracted that vicious old judge.

- So, he started. What is going on that warrants this meeting when you have consistently refused to talk to me for the past few months?

- I want to talk to you about Madeleine.

- Like me," he lied, "Madeleine was obviously the least of your worries. I've been worried ever since she disappeared.

She stared at him and he realized that she was looking for proof of her duplicity on her face. He tried to maintain his mask of honesty as the judge had taught him, hoping he could draw her in, but she didn't seem as gullible as her older sister.

- I think she's been arrested," he announced.

- Yes, so what?

He had been told about the judge's plan and what he was supposed to do next. She was speechless at his lack of surprise.

- Did you know?

- Of course I knew. Madeleine was arrested the day after the drugs were found, didn't you know that?

She nodded and he assumed she had an answer for that, since it was a blatant lie.

- Is she in jail then?

- Not at all," he continued. 'If she was, I wouldn't tell you she was missing. She was only in jail for a few hours. I have a friend, a judge who helped me get her out, at least in part. Then her parents took over and that's when everything went wrong.

- Derailed? How did she get derailed?

- I don't know. My friend couldn't do anything for me anymore: too risky for his position. He could only tell me that it was placed but I don't know anything more.

- Placed?

She was just repeating his words, but he knew that in her head the thoughts were racing. She was considering all possible scenarios and he would help her choose the worst possible one.

- I am terribly worried. I love Madeleine and I know she loves me too. We were going to settle down together and she would never leave me like this without any news. She needs to be locked up somewhere and if not in prison, then somewhere just as horrible.

- An insane asylum," he said.

Inwardly, Jeremy smiled. He was managing to get her exactly where he wanted her.

- Excuse me?" he said, falsely surprised.

- 'I've heard about the possibility of an asylum.

- An asylum? That's not possible. Then she must have been recognized as insane. That means she may never get out.

Her eyes widened again, she had to press her advantage.

- We need to know where she is. If your parents placed her, they must have records showing where she is.

- Not at home, they'd be too scared for me to find them.

Trust reigns, Jerome says, as he welcomes this suspicion.

- Where then?

- In my father's office. It's safe.

- I know. You need a code and a key to get in. I could never get in there alone.

- I know the code.

- And the key?

- I'd give you that too, but I'd have to keep my parents in the dark about it.

- I'd do anything to get them to leave you alone for a day or two.

- Then you'd have a real miracle.

- I can do miracles for Madeleine.

He almost burst out laughing at the expression on her face at that last sentence.

CHAPTER 12

His mother sounded like a funeral. The news that her grandmother had been the victim of a mugging was terrible news in itself, but it came at the time of the exam, so she couldn't take Sarah with her.

- 'We'll only be gone for two days,' her father said. 'Just long enough to make sure your grandmother is well taken care of. We've made arrangements with your aunt for you to stay with her.

- Yes, Dad," she said, but she knew she would never set foot in her aunt's house and would not tell her parents she was away until they returned.

He risked another punishment but at least he had a free hand for two days, which was a lot. He didn't think for a second about the problems Jerome had gone through to achieve this, only his determination mattered.

Once his parents were gone, he searched through his father's papers to find the key to his office. She had no trouble finding it. He took Madeleine's cell phone and immediately called Jerome.

- I have it," he said without preamble.

- Sarah?" came Jerome's voice. Is that you?

- Yes, it is.

- Do you have the key?

- Yes, I have the key.

- Then let's meet again....

- Tonight. In front of the building where my father works. It's too crowded during the day.

- That's fine.

She was determined to stay in control of the situation. Little did she know that by slowing down, she was giving Jerome and his ally time to set their trap.

***

Jerome was waiting, sitting on a stone in front of the large office building. As in their previous meeting, he had taken the precaution of not showing off his newfound wealth so as not to arouse the suspicions of Sarah, who was much smarter than she seemed to think.

The girl arrived when it had already been dark for two hours.

- It's about time," whispered the young man. It's already late.

- I know," she replied. But anyway, for the moment there's nothing we can do. The director is still awake. We'll have to wait until midnight for him to fall asleep.

Jeremy was surprised. He was aware of the night watchman's habits, that he fell asleep every night after midnight, but only because the judge had warned him about this, otherwise he wouldn't have even thought about this detail. This 17-year-old girl had not only thought about it but knew exactly what the habits of the place were. He was more impressed than he would have liked.

So they stayed for almost two hours waiting for the right moment and he played the role set by the judge. They started by talking about Madeleine and of course he appeared concerned and fervent about love, then he cleverly shifted the discussion to Sarah encouraging her to talk about herself and her problems. This strange cocktail worked and he managed to get confessions he never expected. Taking advantage of the revelations the judge extracted from Madeleine, he was able to play on her heartstrings and seem constantly ahead of her thoughts. When midnight struck, he saw in her eyes that he had managed to confuse her more than anyone else ever had. The first part of the plan was a complete success.

***

Entering the building was a real formality, and Jerome thought that one guard to oversee such a place was a real aberration. He then imagined breaking back into the offices, but then changed his mind. Petty theft was no longer his thing; his business was now of a different kind.

They arrived at her father's office and Sarah pulled out the keys she had stolen to open the door. It was a classic no-frills office. Sarah and Madeleine's father was a civil servant of no great stature. Jerome imagined his life and felt like throwing up; he would never accept such a pathetic existence.

They rummaged through shelves and drawers. During this search, Jerome found an object that fascinated him, a weapon. Gun ownership was strictly regulated in the region, and only the police, big crooks, and a privileged few owned them, legally or otherwise. He wondered how Sarah's father had managed to obtain this right and wanted to ask Sarah about it, but he knew it wasn't appropriate. However, he could not resist the temptation and slipped the weapon into his pocket. As soon as he did, Sarah made what she thought was a momentous discovery.

- Look at this!" she said to Jerome, pulling out a small gray shirt.

- What is it? Jerome asked, falsely curious.

- 'It's a bill from a mental institution. It's a room for Madeleine. They had her committed.

Jerome took the papers from him and pretended to read them. He put on his most horrified expression.

- You're right. Obviously she has been committed since she was released. Look, there's the HP decision signed by the judge. And that's not all.

He handed her the last page, the planned shot. It was a handwritten letter signed by the so-called director of this mental institution, recounting a tragic event.

- She had attempted suicide and was now in serious condition.

She screamed and, in a rage, dropped everything on the desk in the center of the room. Jeremy threw himself on top of her to hold her down.

- Stop!" he said to calm her down. You're going to get us spotted.

- She almost died because of them! They locked her up instead of helping her....

- I know, but if we end up in jail, there's nothing we can do for her.

- For her?

She looked at him in disbelief. She put on her 'white knight' expression that had worked so well with her sister.

- All is not lost," he said.

She saw in his eyes that he had taken a step toward her heart, but there was no time to push his lead any further. He led her out of the office, closing in behind him. They left the building in no time.

They found themselves back where they started. Jerome could feel Sarah's nervousness after all these revelations. All those documents left there by a judge-paid maintenance man had really played their role to perfection. It was out of the question to leave it there.

- You said there was still hope," she said suspiciously.

- I already told you I have a friend who is a judge. If he knows of the danger Madeleine is in, he will agree to help me and I could use him to pressure your parents.

He saw her regain hope and, almost to his surprise, threw himself into her arms. Amazed by this gesture, Jeremy decided to take advantage of the opportunity. He kissed her and felt her kiss him back before quickly pushing him away.

- No," she said offensively. That's not fair.

- Yes," she admitted in frustration. I'm sorry. It's the emotion.

He felt her hesitate and feared losing the entire benefit of this evening and he didn't want that.

- 'I'll do everything I can to get Madeleine out of her prison,' he lied fervently, 'and I'll do it quickly. Promise me that you will come to see me tomorrow night at my house, I swear I will have news.

She looked at him for a moment, undecided.

- 'All right,' he admitted. I'll be there.

And with that promise, she disappeared into the night. Jerome didn't insist, but he had made up his mind. He understood why the judge wanted this young woman so badly. She was vivacious, intelligent, and above all, inexperienced. Though brief, their kiss had taught him that she hadn't kissed many boys in her life and he was certain she was still a virgin. That's what the dirty old man wanted, a virgin.

Unfortunately for him, he wasn't going to get what he wanted. Jerome had tasted the forbidden fruit and he intended to go all the way. Tomorrow night, he was going to make a woman out of Sarah Bonnet, whether she liked it or not. He would deal with the judge later, the old man would be as satisfied with the remains as he had been with Madeleine.

***

Theodora Lupa was going through a real ordeal. Lying on her stomach on a wooden table set up in the center of the judge's living room for the occasion, she was being brutally sodomized by the judge's African driver.

The judge had asked her to go to his house in the early evening and she knew this meant another hellish session, but she had never expected what she was about to experience.

As soon as she entered, she found the judge sitting on his couch, dressed in his usual robe. The unfortunate Madeleine who had to put up with this monster every day was next to him, naked as always.

- Get undressed!" the judge ordered her.

Having long since abandoned any inclination to resist, Theodora obeyed without a word and thus found herself also completely naked before this old man. He turned his head to the small wooden table and she saw that he had installed straps on it. He shuddered but moved toward her.

- Lie down on your stomach!

The judge continued to address her politely, but always using an imperious tone to command her as one would a small dog. He liked to play on paradoxes with her in this way. He sat down on the table and saw that the straps were meant to go around her neck and hands, provided she put her arms at her sides. Without a word Madeleine crawled towards her and imprisoned her. Theodora found herself totally helpless, ready to suffer the assaults of the old libertine without being able to resist. But he did not move and instead it was Madeleine who came back to him and, spreading the flaps of her robe, began to fellatio him. Theodora was beginning to think she was destined to be an ornamental object when she felt a presence behind her, a huge shadow resting on her. She strained against the strap that imprisoned her to try to see behind her and was able to make out the black giant standing behind her, naked. She screamed when she realized what was about to happen.

* * *

The judge was enjoying the spectacle of Kono ravaging Theodora's insides. The Congolese giant, with his imposing sex, had begun to work on the ring of this haughty bourgeois, who immediately began to scream and beg; to no avail, of course. As the black sex began to work its way into his bowels, his screams became shrill and the judge's erection, encouraged by the work of an increasingly experienced Madeleine, became stronger. The judge had never sodomized Theodora and thought that she was a virgin by this orifice which must have made this first experience even more traumatic for her. With an impassive face, Kono slowly but surely sank into her without caring for a second about his victim's screams. The judge could see the immense piece of flesh gradually disappearing between Theodora's buttocks and if he hadn't already witnessed such a spectacle, he would have doubted that he could penetrate her completely.

Unfortunately for Theodora, Kono would only stop once the sodomy was completely consumed. The latter screamed louder and louder, pulling at the straps that imprisoned her, but they were made of a particularly strong leather and she would not be able to free herself. The worst thing was that Kono had finally managed to completely fuck the poor woman. She turned to the judge who merely nodded. Kono then began her back and forth motion and

Theodora, who thought she had been through hell while being fucked, literally exploded. Her anus bleeding, her eyes filled with tears, she suffered this horror as she screamed louder and louder and cursed the name of the judge who laughed at her.

Caught up in his pleasure, he leaned down to the little whore between his thighs.

- 'I hope you're warm, my little Madeleine,' he said, 'because you're next.'

She felt Madeleine's teeth clench on her sex in terror and laughed.

***

Kono did not sodomize Madeleine that night. He left Theodora completely devastated, still tied to the wooden table. As soon as the huge sex was removed from her bleeding anus, the unfortunate woman fell unconscious and the judge ordered Madeleine to take a shower. After the terror she had endured, the thought of only being sodomized by the old man's normally constituted sex was almost a relief. She turned on the water and waited, increasingly anxious, for the judge's intrusion; an intrusion that never came. For the first time since she had become the judge's plaything, Madeleine finished a shower without finding herself bent in half, a cock frozen in her anus. She took it as a gift and stepped out of the shower with a smile. Her smile faded when she heard the judge call her into the living room and imagined herself facing the black driver. Hesitating, she wanted to curl up at the foot of the bed, but knew it would be unnecessary protection.

Trembling, she passed through the door to her room and saw, relieved, that Kono had not returned. Theodora was still bound and unconscious. The judge was facing his television screen and was watching a video that seemed to fascinate him.

- Come here, my child," he said. This will interest you.

She approached and was not surprised to find that it was a porno film. A young couple were making love in a small, discreet room, nothing special. Yet she found it strange, the room seemed familiar and the man reminded her of someone. Her heart stopped when she realized it was Jerome, her Jerome, having sex in her apartment. The judge saw that she understood.

- Your boyfriend isn't bored either and that's not all.

She pressed the remote and the image changed. It was the same room but the couple was different. Jeremy was still there with another girl. The judge pressed again and it was a third girl. Madeleine shouted.

- Your boyfriend replaced you quickly and not just once," the judge continued. And he intends to continue. I can also tell you the name of his next conquest, you know her very well: Sarah, your little sister.

This was too much for Madeleine, she got angry. She grabbed the phone that was right next to her and hit the judge hard on the head. The judge, who was clearly not expecting this, collapsed. Madeleine then picked up Theodora's clothes from the floor and ran for the door. She wanted to get away from this hellish place, away from this monster.

She crossed the corridor convinced that before reaching the door she would be grabbed by the black giant who would take her back to the room where she would be severely punished, but she wanted to try her luck. The door was only two meters away... one meter... she put her hand on the handle and pressed it to emerge in the corridor, free. She ran to the elevator and called it. It opened almost immediately and she stepped inside. As he descended, she dressed, not caring that the clothes were not quite her size. Then the elevator doors opened and she was able to walk out into the street and disappear into the night.